Point Illusion

Seneka Ecks

Copyright © 2016 by Seneka Ecks

All Rights Reserved

This book is a work of fiction. Names, characters, places, and incidents are the product of the author's imagination or are used fictitiously. Any resemblance to actual events, locales, or persons, living or dead, is entirely coincidental.

Acknowledgements

To Glenn, for creating the time and space required, which led to the opportunity to see this through to completion.

To Nathan and Jose, who should already be famous, in my humble opinion, for providing a level of insight and guidance of which all creative types would be jealous.

To John at Forensic Technologies, for making sure what I wrote was theoretically possible, technically accurate, culturally graceful – and of course truthful.

To the real "Weetco", who really did make a difference in my life back then, and still is now.

To a family who understands and unconditionally accepts consequences

a sailboat, by the way. Yes, it has an engine, but if you're in a hurry to get somewhere, you're not on a sailboat anyway, so it's a small engine as far as boats go, about thirty-five horses. Which is enough to get around in harbors and channels and places like that. But before you judge, keep in mind that, technically, I could sail around the world on just one tank of gas, or diesel, in the Carillion's case. It might take a while, but it's feasible.

    He told me his name was Pete, but I doubted it as soon as the name came out of his mouth. It didn't matter. This was a short run. I picked him up in San Pedro (pronounced by the locals as *Peedro*, by the way), and was taking him up the coast of Southern California to a city called Redondo Beach. By car, that's about a twelve mile drive up Highway One. By boat, it was just under twenty-five miles, or about twenty-one nautical miles, to be pedantic. But I'm pretty sure it was how Pete got to Redondo that was important to him. Because it took us about four and a half hours on the Carillion. He didn't complain about the time.

    He did get seasick, though. And let me tell you right here you can never judge a person by whether or not they hold their bucket on the water. It has nothing to do with demographics such as race or sex or age, or with any of those socially admired qualities like virility, will, integrity, perseverance or grit. I've seen filthy rich seasoned sailors with twenty years of blue-water ocean experience succumb to the sickness in calm waters on a bright, sunny day. And as you might expect, I've been at the helm when people who have never set foot aboard a boat in their life get caught in a localized squall with steep and frothing seven-foot swells that pitch the boat violently in every direction, and right after, eat room temperature, twelve-hour old store-bought sushi out of a plastic bag, and swear right there on the deck of the Carillion they were quitting their jobs so they could spend the rest of their life on a boat. There's just no telling. The tell, really, is how they handle it. It's a character thing, something about being willing to admit you're sick as a dog because you're on a boat.

So as soon as Pete started talking about how it must have been last night's dinner that was making him so sick, I was pretty sure his real name wasn't Pete. Not that Pete talked much in our four hours together. He had something else on his mind, clearly – I mean aside from being green – and I'm pretty sure it had something to do with whatever was inside the green and gold gym bag he refused to let go of for the entire trip.

It hardly mattered, because we were pulling up to the public dock at Redondo Beach. I could tell by his look and his pace that he had already seen whatever it was he was expecting to see on land, and he could not wait to get off the Carillion. Which is a common thing. I think it's fair to say there are two types of people in this world: the ones who see sailing as an agonizingly slow way to get somewhere – or nowhere – and the ones who see it as a journey of the mind. Pete was of the former type. And just as soon as I had the boat kissed up to the public dock, Pete bolted for dry land, gym bag in hand, but not before handing me an envelope. We hadn't discussed the charges, but I could tell by the bulk of the envelope that it was enough. Unless they were all ones, and even then, the client had at least covered the fuel cost. Round trip. So at worst, I had broken even on this run.

What Pete was expecting to see, or at least the car he slipped into on the passenger side, was a shiny black Mercedes S500 perched on a fresh black asphalt public parking area about a hundred feet up a powder blue wooden gangplank from the dock. The car was one of the AMG types. It had dealer tags for license plates, so it must have been new. It looked it. I hadn't even switched off the engine or secured the boat to the dock before the Mercedes was backing out of its parking spot. Which was when I realized I wouldn't be staying in Redondo Beach: Pete and the gym bag were already gone.

The only vessel close to me on the public dock was about thirty feet ahead of my bow, so with the Carillion drifting gently and harmlessly away from the dock, I opened the envelope and counted out twelve hundred dollars, all in crisp, clean hundreds. So I figured whatever Pete's profession was, the gym bag had something to do with it, and it was probably illegal. If this were the case, and had we been boarded by the Coast Guard while in transit, I would have gone back to prison, as would have Pete. So twelve hundred dollars was a fair price, I guess, what with the risk and all.

I don't advertise my services. There's no boat-for-hire website with my name and a picture of the Carillion on it. I have enough referral business to keep me just as busy as I want to be, which honestly isn't that busy. Pete was a referral, I think. He said the right name over the phone when he was booking the boat, so I just took it for granted he was legit. Not in the legal sense of the word, but in the referral sense.

Penny Page started the whole referral thing for me, and if you keep up with the electronic dance music scene, you probably recognize the name. There was a song about four years ago with a hook that stated she wished to do it more but we might think she was a whore, followed by another line that told us she liked to shake her butt but when she did, got called a slut. Or something like that. It shot to number two on the dance charts and stayed within the top five for more than a month. That was Penny Page, and singing those confessions to a pulsing one hundred forty drum and bass beats per minute had made her both popular and rich. I knew her before all that, before she was Penny Page.

I am what is called a liveaboard, which means I reside on the Carillion. It's a lot like living in an RV. They're about the same size in length and width, and have just about the same amenities, which makes living on her, well, livable. I try not to spend a lot of time on land. Just to the grocery store or bank and back, maybe twice a month. But in this instance, I had driven to the city of Downey to pick up a part for the

Carillion's engine, a raw water impeller blade. At the time, the boat was slipped at Long Beach, another city along the coast of California. Downey was north and inland by about fifteen miles. Fifteen miles on land usually isn't such a big deal. The freeways of southern California, on the other hand, can be a huge deal. And on this particular evening, the southbound 710 freeway was slammed with a triple whammy of rush hour, construction work, and an accident with injuries. So I did what everybody else does in SoCal when the freeways don't live up to their name: I take surface streets. Which worked really well until I got into downtown Long Beach, which, it turns out, is quite a popular place to be on Thursday nights: nightclubs, bars, restaurants. Which meant even the city streets were jammed. So I did what everyone else does when the surface streets are jammed, and took an even more obscure route which, as is usually the case, took me into an older, more unkempt and less-traveled part of the city.

Which was when I discovered Penny Page. She probably wasn't old enough legally to be drinking at the time, but there was no doubt she was drunk. So drunk she was passed out. On the sidewalk. In front of a liquor store, but I'm pretty sure her precise location at the time had little to do with an intent to purchase more alcohol. I'm not entirely sure, because I was about thirty feet away at the time, sitting in my car at a stop light waiting for the green. There were two other girls standing over the prone Penny, and they seemed to be upset with her. One of them said 'Fuck this bitch' – I heard that – and then the other girl threw something down on top of Penny. It looked like maybe a purse. And then they left. They just walked away, down the street, around the corner and out of sight.

Please don't think I'm a Good Samaritan. I'm whatever the opposite of that would be. Remember, I spent some time behind bars, and a small part of the reason I got sent there was for being something similar to a Good Samaritan. But I couldn't just drive on with a young girl sprawled on the sidewalk in downtown Long Beach at nine o'clock on a Thursday night. Nobody's that much of an asshole – or pussy – right? So I flipped a U-turn and pulled up next to the liquor store. No one was running to her aid. This wasn't in front of some throbbing nightclub or popular dining destination. It was a side street liquor store dating to the fifties and retrofitted with the option of buzzing patrons in through a bullet-proof glass and iron-barred front door. Those inside the liquor store probably didn't know she was out there. Or would care if they did. This was a part of downtown Long Beach where the sight of people passed out on the sidewalk was not an unusual one. She was just plain alone. Except for me.

It turns out she wasn't passed out, but she was close, and was definitely crying. Or sobbing. You know, the way drunks sob and babble and moan for whatever reason they have for that. I've been there. Not recently, of course, but I recognized the pattern and could recall with very little imagination all the tortuous steps this poor girl had taken to get to the point where she was face down drunk on a sidewalk, puking and sobbing.

The real problem was her ass.

She was wearing something like a dress that was black and already pretty short, and apparently on her unplanned journey to the sidewalk, the dress had hiked up, leaving the whole world to see Penny's ass and nothing else except a pair of bright pink thong underwear. Suddenly I was a Good Samaritan, again. I mean, I don't have any children, but I figured this was probably somebody's little girl at some point in the past, and if she were my little girl, I would expect that if some stranger were to come along and find her in this predicament, that stranger would be a Good Samaritan, even if being so was against his or her better judgment. Even if that stranger were an ex-felon.

My first thought was to just tug the dress back down to cover her up, but then I imagined what that might look like to someone else – as in *what's that pervert doing to that defenseless girl* – so I forced myself not to look at the bright pink and pale flesh combination and just asked her if she needed any help. And, of course, like all good drunks, Penny sobbed out that she wanted to go home. *I waa-aa guh huuum.* That made perfect sense to me, so with relatively little effort, considering she weighed a grand total of perhaps a hundred twenty pounds, I loaded Penny into the front seat of my Rabbit, ensuring, of course, that both she and the dress were restored to socially acceptable standards, an act that required significantly more effort. And restraint.

Her shoes were nowhere to be found, but that item one of the girls had thrown down did turn out to be Penny's purse. It was a small black thing held shut by an embedded magnet, but had just enough room for a cluster of plastic cards held together by an elastic hair tie, a tampon, some gum, a set of earrings, a ceramic pot pipe that looked like it had never been used, and a phone charger. No phone. So I checked the sidewalk where I had found her. I even went in to the liquor store and asked, but no one had left a phone, so I gave up looking and returned to the car and the young blonde stranger slumped in its front seat, who was still sobbing behind closed eyes, but in brief murmurs that were more cute than annoying.

She had also thrown up by then.

In my car.

Naturally. Like that goes with being a Good Samaritan.

Doing the right thing always comes with consequences.

Chapter Two

All the cards, which were mostly department store charge cards, had the name Penelope Colski embossed on it, including the driver's license, from which I learned two things immediately: the face in the picture on the driver's ID was of the girl in my front seat, minus the tear-streaked eyeliner and mascara, the puffiness, and the stubbornly clinging remnants of glitter. The second thing was the ID was issued by the state of Illinois. Which was when I realized I might not be driving Penny home. At least not that night.

So I took her to my home, which was a boat called the Carillion floating in a slip a couple miles away. She couldn't walk, naturally, so I hoisted her over one shoulder and carried her down the floating dock to the boat like a fireman carries someone out of a burning house, except I doubt people being rescued from burning houses have vomit all over them. I don't know. That was the least of my problems. Even though this was a relatively unpopulated part of town, it still had to look suspicious – to anyone – as I carried what could have been a dead body over my shoulder towards a boat in a marina in Long Beach at ten o'clock at night. Which is a large part of the reason why I'm a liveaboard: anyone who's on the docks that time of night isn't asking questions.

I'd been drunk like that before, too many times, so I knew it would be around four hours before the chemistry in the girl's brain would be normalized enough to begin wondering what was what. So I pressed a carafe of coffee for myself and, seated at the boat's navigation station, used my laptop's internet to try to find out what I could about anyone named Penelope Colski, while the girl with that name slept it off in the boat's forward v-berth. Colski, it turns out, is not so common a name, and no definitive hits popped out. Google produced hits naturally, over twenty-three thousand for the surname, but only forty-three, amazingly, when joined with either Penny or Penelope, none of which further illuminated the girl's immediate fate. So I did a little research on the address found on her Illinois driver's license, which was a street named Ashland in a town called Evanston, and I actually got excited for a moment when Google maps revealed a Penny Park on that street. But I figured that was just a coincidence, and learned little else, except that Evanston was a cozy little town of neat, single-family homes with front and back yards covered mostly in green grass, and that it had changed very little in the past fifty years or so, except for the demographics. Had I known the girl had already changed her last name, at least on the Internet, to Page, I would have most likely stumbled across a wealth of data via social media sites, several to which Penny was subscribed, and would have therefore solved at least one problem that night. But I didn't know of it, so I instead wasted my time learning more about the various suburb cities of Chicago until I dozed off, still seated at the nav station.

About four hours later I woke up to find Penny Colski pointing a flare gun at my nose. It wasn't loaded, but I didn't let her know that until about a year later. Of all the reasons this girl had to either love or hate me at three o'clock of that morning, her most immediate and persuading impression was that at least I wasn't a creep, the premise of said impression being the presumptive fact that I had not taken advantage of her. I told her she had been too drunk to have remembered if I had. She rejected this assertion until I challenged her to describe where the two of us had met that boost, part of Perry's sales pitch, intended to soften me up, make me feel good about me. So I would listen more carefully, and most likely catch whatever it was he was pitching. If it ever seems like magic, it's the magic of the sea that is at work, not some ex-felon with a salvaged sailboat named after a spaceship from the Star Wars movies.

Now, the other thing. Trippy is not my real name. It has nothing to do with me being the third in line of a family succession of names. My father wasn't a junior, and my grandfather wasn't a senior. I'm called Trippy for a much stupider reason. Growing up, I had a real problem learning to walk. It persisted, and even at the age of nine, I would still stumble and fall on occasion, usually in public places for all to see. Part of it turned out to be my mother's fault, who insisted I wear pants that had been handed down, pants that were too long in the inseam. She'd roll them up to compensate for their length, but me being a boy, I'd always end up doing something boyish that unraveled those folds to the point where they would impede my ability to walk. So I tripped a lot in those early formative years, and the nickname, vigorously promoted by family and friends, stuck. I made the mistake of sharing this story with Penny Colski over that long weekend years ago, and had she never become Penny Page, people like Perry Jennison would be calling me Frank, which is my given name. I walk just fine now, but people who think they like me insist on calling me Trippy.

"Is it high profile?" I asked Perry. Needing me to work my magic meant Perry had a client he wanted me to take sailing. Usually somebody exceedingly stoned or high or troublesome or in trouble or about to throw a tantrum that would lead to trouble. And there was usually money involved. Somebody else's money, and that somebody else didn't want that money being frittered away on tantrum-prone, spoiled rotten mega-dicks who were refusing to cooperate just because they could. Which was when that somebody else with all the money would call Perry.

Who the client is makes a huge difference in my life. I'm not a fan of the media. Lots of Perry's people are. Oscar Wilde has that famous saying about the only thing worse than being talked about is not being talked about. Media equals publicity. As a general rule, ex-felons don't like publicity. Or the media. So I wanted to know what I might be getting myself into. If Perry's client was a Miley or a Bieber or some other high-profile, problem-prone diva, I would have to weigh the consequences. Carefully. Which was why I had asked the question of Perry.

"No. He's a finance guy. With problems," said Perry.

'Problems' usually meant some sort of addiction, but I wanted to hear it from Perry.

"Like?"

"Not the usual stuff," he said. "The guy just closed a big merger between two tech firms. Worth billions. And now he's freaking out. Falling apart. You know, Howard Hughes, hiding in the bedroom, missing work, not shaving; thinks he's worthless, thinks they're coming to get him."

"How did he come to you?"

"His wife read about you in People magazine."

"Christ."

"Yeah. The Penny Page article from 2012. The mystery man who saved her soul. The wife contacted my office."

"Christ," I said again. I was aware of the article but had never read it. Didn't want to. It was not a specific reference to me, and most readers at the time thought Adam Jack was the mystery man, because he and Penny were romantically involved when the mag hit the stands, so it never became a big deal in my life. In fact, guys like Perry Jennison worked hard to make sure it remained mysterious, mostly because it was good publicity, but not for me, and I was quite comfortable with it working both ways like that.

"Sounds like what he needs is a little therapy," I said.

complicated than it really is. Being twenty miles wide, just about anyone leaving from the greater Los Angeles area could point the boat at two-ten on the compass until they saw the island, at which point they could make a right and just sail until there was no more island, even on an overcast day. And this being the seventeenth of May, it was. May gray, the TV weather celebs call it. Or June gloom. Not a fan of cheap rhymes like that. Actually, it's the existence of the marine layer that leads to the clouds, and thus the overcast conditions. None of which matters to a compass needle or, in my case, a handheld GPS unit, which was all anyone needed, honestly. That, and a chart, and you can't go wrong. Thanks to computers and satellites, the days of plotting courses, drawing lines and measuring distances are pretty much over. I can still navigate that way, but find it easier just to use the technology.

At fifteen minutes before ten o'clock, I decided to head up to the marina's parking lot to wait for the finance guy with problems, and his wife. I hadn't bothered to ask Perry if the wife was coming with us, but it wouldn't matter; I've done couples before. Sometimes it helps having the spouse or life partner there. Sometimes you end up with two sick people, or two addicted people, or two angry people. I've seen it all. Up close. But couples or not, it seems to reassure clients when they arrive at the marina if there's someone there to greet them, tell them where to park, what to bring, all that stuff.

There was a small knot of people gathered just on the other side of the gate that separates the parking area from the boat slips, and one of them was Redman. They were all looking off to the left, so naturally I looked in that direction and discovered what was so fascinating that morning. About two hundred feet further down the parking lot a fire truck, two police cars, and an ambulance, all of them with their lights flashing, were huddled around something I couldn't see. I stepped through the gate and stood next to Redman.

When Redman saw me he said, "Murder."

"How do you know that?" I asked, and then noticed that Redman had cleaned himself up, or at least shaved, and his shirt looked fresh. Quite wrinkled, but it looked clean. It was an improvement.

He pointed to the commotion of flashing red and blue lights. "The two unmarked cars, to the right. See 'em?"

I did.

"Homicide investigation," said Redman.

I didn't know if they were homicide cops, but trusted Redman on matters such as these. Because he's a sailing derelict, and would know.

"Nice," I said, "Right in our backyard. And I got clients coming."

As if on cue, a uniformed officer began cordoning off a section of the parking lot with that yellow crime tape. Like the kind you see on the cop shows. Which was what this felt like to me, a drama, an episode of something. And I was drawn to it.

"Maybe they're filming a TV show," I said.

"Show me the camera," said Redman. He then turned to me. "Do you know how many people it takes to film something like that? You got actors, producers, at least one director, makeup, wardrobe, the camera guys, the electrical guys, the lighting guys, and usually a few rent-a-cops hanging around to keep guys like me from crashing the party. Plus all the trucks to carry all that shit. Thus the phrase, 'major production'. Nope, this is a murder."

I was still gawking at the drama but said, "Point taken."

"Anyone famous?" said Redman.

"How would I know?"

"You don't know who your clients are?"

I looked to Redman. "Oh. I thought you were talking about the murder."

"Naturally," Redman said, smiling.

"No, not famous, just some finance guy. And his wife."

Which reminded me that they were the reason I had come up to the parking lot. I checked my watch and then shifted my attention in the opposite direction of the police drama, to the right, towards the parking lot's main entrance, and began scanning for a car that didn't belong there. That sounds dumb, but I was pretty good at picking out the kind of cars my clients arrived in. They weren't Civics or Corollas or Oldsmobiles. Maybe a Prius, but more likely they'd arrive in a Mercedes or a BMW or something even more exotic. So that's what I was looking for when I spotted the same black AMG Mercedes I thought I had seen in the Redondo Beach parking lot. The one I saw Pete getting into. No plates, just the dealer tags. It was identical. Had to be a coincidence. Black Mercedes were a popular car here in LA. Likely dozens of them floating around. Or maybe it was Pete's ride. After all, this was where we had initially met. No reason why he wouldn't have come back here. For some other reason, maybe.

Then I heard Redman saying, "Maybe that's them."

I looked to him, and then to where he was pointing. It was a powder blue marina maintenance building with a composite roof about two hundred feet away from where we were standing. There was a black couple standing on the sidewalk in front of the structure, the man with both arms wrapped around the woman's shoulders. Like he was keeping her warm or something. Like they were huddled together. I wondered. I had assumed that a finance guy named Trent would be white, and quickly realized how wrong – and how stupid – that assumption might be. I've never considered myself a racist, but my thinking was obviously prejudiced. Because I'm white. So naturally, all finance guys named Trent have to be white, too, right? Idiot. I should have googled the name. If he's putting together business mergers worth billions, he's probably high profile enough to have a picture somewhere on the Internet. Linked in, or something.

Now I had no choice. Now I had to walk over there and tell this guy that I thought the guy I was looking for was white because his name was Trent, and Trent sounds like a white name. Such a racist. I started walking towards them, and on the way began my prejudiced profile: type of clothing, quality of shoes, value of jewelry, watch, sunglasses, style of haircut. More than fifty feet away I realized this was not a homeless couple. Clean, crisp creases in the guy's pants, and that little cuff at the bottom, just above a pair of really nice deck shoes. They looked like Varvatos's, which run a couple hundred bucks a pair. Which was what I would wear if I could afford it. The girl had on a pair of tight-fitting stone-washed jeans and bright yellow running shoes with pink shoelaces. They were both wearing dark green insulated nylon windbreakers.

As I got closer to the two, and it became apparent to them that my course would intersect with their location, a look of apprehension grew on the man's face. I was dressed in a pair of Levi's, a white t-shirt that advertised some bar in Mazatlán, and a pair of forty-dollar deck shoes. But I had shaved that morning, so I didn't look too much like a creep. But the guy didn't know that. To him, I was an approaching stranger, and therefore a potential threat. So I put on what I thought was a genuine, reassuring smile, and slowed my pace.

I stopped about ten feet in front of them. "Are you the Haydens, by any chance?" I said, still smiling.

They both relaxed, and the guy dropped his arms from around the girl's shoulders. He then smiled awkwardly and extended a hand. "I'm Trent."

I introduced myself as I shook his hand, using my nickname, as I was sure that was how Perry had described me. Thereafter I learned that Trent's wife's name was Darcy, and shook her hand. Trent and Darcy Hayden. Go figure. What shocked me the most was their ages. Both of them would get carded in a bar. Even in this part of town. I wasn't even sure they were old enough to vote.

"You guys ready to do some sailing?" I asked, a standard opening line that I used a lot.

Trent looked to his wife, and they smiled at each other. "Darcy's decided to stay on shore," said Trent, still adoringly focused on his wife.

Which was when I knew this would be a piece of cake. These two people loved each other madly, you could just tell. And people in love generally don't do destructive things, to each other, to themselves, or to the world. Well, okay, that's not a true statement at all, and I have two ex-wives dying to prove just how untrue it is. But for the moment I was taking it as a truth that I hoped would persist for the next forty-eight or so hours. Despite my checkered and uncouth past, I'm not a bad judge of character, or maybe because of it, and that judgment was leaning heavily towards kindness, sympathy, and understanding in regards Trent Hayden. And his wife, Darcy.

We walked over to their car, which turned out to be a Tesla, of course, and I sadly spouted my envy and admiration at the electric marvel. As Trent pulled an overnight bag out of the car's trunk, he told me it was a rental but that he wouldn't mind owning one. I was wondering how much it would set me back to rent one for myself, you know, just to impress someone, but in the same thought realized I had no one to impress, so dropped the fantasy. Darcy joined Trent at the car's trunk, and after seeing the look in her eye, recognized this was about to become the goodbye moment. I sauntered a few respectful feet away from the couple and half-turned away, but I could still hear their words: *be safe; don't worry, I will; keep an open mind; you know I always do*, each loving admonition and its response punctuated with a kiss or an embrace or a deeply-stared look of reassurance and belief. That made me more jealous than the car did. I had had four phenomenally great romantic relationships in my forty-plus years, but was currently involved exclusively with a boat, and this demonstration was reminding me just how splendid human relationships could be. Maybe I had one more in me. Besides the Carillion.

Chapter Six

Trent wanted to wait until his wife had left the parking lot in the rented Tesla before we started walking to the gate that led to the slip holding the Carillion. As we passed the small cluster of lookers who had persisted in gawking at the police affair further down the parking lot, Redman turned and greeted me. I knew what he was doing; he wanted to meet the client.

"*The* Trent Hayden of Sandfall Paradigm?" asked Redman, after I had introduced him to Trent.

"Yes," said Trent, subdued. He and I walked through the gate and towards the boats. Redman followed.

"I was just reading about your sorting algorithm; the Group of Eights; isn't that what you call it?

"That's what Sandfall named it."

"It's basically a modified Schwarzian transform. Except that your algo makes a predictable skip in calling to the element every eighth recursion. Brilliant. It's not always correct – because of the skip – but often enough. And incredibly fast."

"Red," I said, "We're going sailing today. Like a day off for Trent, so…"

"You don't understand, Trippy. It's predictably wrong. *Predictably*. Which means it's never wrong, because the code can predict when it will be wrong and--"

I had stopped walking and was staring at Redman, as menacing a stare as I could manage, considering his enthusiasm. If this were a rock star or a famous actor, Redman would have stayed up in the parking lot with the gawkers. But guys like Trent were the rock stars in Redman's world. I tried to keep that in mind as my eyes told Redman to shut up.

Trent had already figured all of this out and said, "You should come up to the lab sometime, Mr. Redman. We're about to wrap up the beta phase, which is usually pretty exciting." He smiled.

Redman's expression looked as though one of us had just slapped him across the face. He stayed straight-faced silent, alternating his look between Trent and myself. Then he began nodding his head and as he did so, said, "Nice try, Hayden. And get me all entangled in it, and all hopeful and promising and applicable until I'm the one that finds the flaw, the weakness, the soft spot, the unsolvable problem that will get me even more wrapped up in it. Until it takes over my life. Enslaved, just like you are, to the point where you can't think straight anymore. Because it's not perfect, but seems like it should be, or could be, and so it's all on you to figure it out and fix it. But you can't. Because it's perfectly imperfect. Just like everything else in this universe."

Redman looked to me and held up his index finger, like he was about to make some final point, or a warning, or a doomsday prediction, but instead just turned around and headed back up the walkway, back towards the gathering of onlookers on the other side of the gate in the parking lot.

After a brief moment of awkward silence, Trent looked to me but was smiling. Like he knew. We started walking again, slowly at first, towards the Carillion's slip.

"Sorry about that," I said. "Red gets a little carried away sometimes."

"Oh, I'm used to it," said Trent. "It's called passion. Seen it before. It kind of goes with the territory in my line of work."

"I thought your line of work was finance," I said.

Trent laughed quietly. "I guess it is. Now."

He left it at that, so I did, too.

When we arrived at the Carillion, the first words out of Trent's mouth were, "It's beautiful," which kind of shocked me. The Carillion doesn't stand out at a marina. She looks pretty much like all the other sailboats there, except older. She's a faded and sun-bleached white, has a single mast about sixty feet high, and sports an equally faded and fraying blue canopy that covers the entrance to the cabin below. It's called a dodger, as in a place you can duck in to dodge the weather. Granted, I keep the Carillion neat and clean, but calling her beautiful is something a prospective buyer might do, a first-time buyer. This might have been the first client who had ever called her beautiful.

I had backed her into the slip because it made access through the cockpit a little more direct. There are two boats per slip in this marina, and only one finger that branches off on either side of the main walkway per slip. If I had put her in bow first, getting onboard would have been over the port side. She was set up for starboard entry. Trent had stopped in his tracks at the Carillion's stern, stuck in adoration mode, his eyes saturated in the vessel's details. He had one of those boyish smiles pressed onto his face, the goofy kind, mouth partly open, held tilted back on its axis.

"Wanna come aboard?" I asked.

"It's sloop-rigged," he said, apparently ignoring me. "About thirty-eight feet, length overall. Lots of freeboard, which means she's forgiving."

"Thirty-six, actually," I said. He was using phrases specific to the world of sailing, which surprised me. Freeboard is the distance from the boat's waterline to the lip of the deck. The less freeboard, the faster the boat, the more of it, increased stability in high seas. Not exactly common knowledge. "You've sailed before, Trent?"

"Never."

My brain said *huh* to his answer, but I said nothing. You don't know details like the freeboard measurement of a sailing vessel if you've never sailed before. Then I remembered who I was dealing with. The way Redman had been so eager to worship this guy, his intelligence. Trent had done his homework. Read a few books, skimmed some magazines, visited websites. This is a good thing. Remember I said there were two types of people when it came to sailing? Indifference can be a bitch. It makes my job as skipper more difficult. It means I'm doing everything under sail. Indifferent clients are just dead weight who tend to get in the way, not ask questions, or ask the wrong kind, the whiny kind: *are we there, yet? Why are we going so slow?* Trent was going to be the other kind. Hands-on. Give him the wheel and make sure he doesn't put the sails in the water. Outstanding. Easy money. A pleasure cruise.

So once I convinced him to step aboard, going through the usual spiel of what's what on a boat was effortless. Ropes are referred to as lines or sheets, sails are called sails, the foremost is the jib, the large one hanging off the mast is the main. That's the boom. It moves around a lot; don't let it hit you in the head. This is the wheel, as in steering; it's located in the cockpit; that's the compass; that digital thing tells you your speed in water, the other one reports water depth. Trent's brain was like a paper towel on spilled water. He not only got it, but was ready to apply it. Dying to.

We started the engine. I like to let the Carillion's engine get close to operating temperature before putting it into action, so I used the five or so minutes to quickly tutor Trent on the mechanics of steering a sailboat. Which was a waste of time, because Trent had apparently read up on that as well, and it's not exactly rocket science anyway: boats steer pretty much the same as cars, especially when they have a steering wheel, as opposed to a tiller. The Carillion has a shiny, chrome wheel that's three feet in diameter. You want to go left, turn the wheel left. Just like a car. Of course Trent began talking about the differential dynamics involved when the steerage occurs at the rear of the vessel, not at the front, like cars. He used the word 'fulcrum', with enthusiasm, by the way as he explained it to me, and I pretended to understand what he was saying.

Two completely unrelated events then occurred. The first was in my head. Trent Hayden was acting completely normal. He didn't appear stressed or nervous or falling apart at the seams, as Perry had described him. Sure, maybe he was under a lot of pressure at work, but that stress had not manifested itself as abnormal or destructive behavior patterns. At least not that I had seen yet. And I know, we had the whole weekend in front of us, but I had seen enough clients step on and off this boat to be fairly confident that Trent Hayden was not about to explode. Just the opposite. He was relaxed, conversant, attentive, rational, all those good things. Like I said, I'm a pretty good judge of character. And that bothered me. Either Trent was masking his true feelings incredibly well, and therefore posed a significant threat to the two of us – and the boat – or Perry had misrepresented him. I've known Perry a long time; he's never lied to me. Has no reason to. My role in his schemes is too important to Perry for him to risk it. So I began wondering what was really going on here. In my mind I replayed the tender scene at the car between Trent and his wife; the way he first shook my hand; his diplomatic and patient interaction with Redman when his wires got crossed. It just didn't add up. So, naturally, I began to worry.

The second event was much more serious. The engine was warmed up, the boat was ready to go, so we were casting off, which is where you release the lines securing the boat to the dock. It's a big deal for first-timers, so I explained the procedure to Trent before we actually did anything. He would step off the boat, go to the point where the stern of the boat was attached to the dock, untie that line, and then hop back aboard the Carillion. It's a short trip from the stern mooring line back to the boat's cockpit, so it's safe to let the rookies handle that one. Just don't let go of the line in your hand, I told him, and if the boat starts to drift away while you're still on land, just pull that line in, bring the boat back to you, and hop onboard. It all happens in slow motion anyway, I explained, because when you're in the slip, there's not much current acting on the boat. Remember, the boat's floating on the water, I told him. Most of the time you untie the line and the boat just sits there, patiently waiting. Meanwhile, I would do the same at the bow, where the other mooring line meets the dock. Because the bow line is further away from the cockpit, it takes just a little more finesse to manage to release the line then walk back to the cockpit to board the craft, and that's why I let the rookies handle the stern line.

Everything went just fine. Trent stepped off the boat, untied the stern mooring line like he'd been performing the act for years, and lithely stepped back aboard. I headed to the bow of the boat, untied the bow line and noticed a green and gold gym bag slouched halfway on the starboard side of the Carillion's bow, the other half hanging limply over the side of the boat. It looked wet, but I still recognized it immediately as the gym bag belonging to Pete, the alleged gang member I had transported to Redondo Beach only yesterday. The gym bag allegedly loaded with something illegal that he had kept clutched in his hand for the entire trip. And I know he had departed with it, still clenched in said hand. Saw it with my own eyes. Saw him get into the black Mercedes with it. Christ, the same Mercedes I might have seen in my parking lot this morning. So what was it doing back onboard the Carillion?

Meanwhile the Carillion was no longer tethered to the dock and my brain was frozen on the implications of the gym bag, specifically its contents.

"Now what do I do?" asked Trent, who was already standing at the wheel, his hands white-knuckle-locked into the ten and two position. I kept hold of the bow line for as long as it reached as I walked back to the cockpit entry, then flipped it aboard and jumped on. First things first, I told myself.

"Okay, which one's the shifter and which one's the throttle?" I asked.

"C'mon, Trippy! You think I wasn't paying attention?" He tapped the chromed lever mounted on the left side of the wheel housing. "Transmission. Push forward for forward, pull back for reverse. Neutral's in the middle." He grabbed hold of its symmetric counterpart on the right side, and goosed the throttle causing the Carillion's engine to gently rev up briefly. "Throttle."

"Okay," I said. Put her into gear and make a left out of the slip."

"Aye, aye, captain. Port bearing, steady as she goes," Trent said, like a kid who's always dreamed of being in control of the starship Enterprise. His wife would be proud.

I kept watch until Trent had negotiated the turn out of the slip without clipping another boat and was centered in the middle of the channel heading out to sea.

"What's our speed, Mr. Hayden?" I said, playing the part.

Trent scanned the array of digital displays in front of him. "One knot, captain."

"Very good. Keep it below three until we clear the breakwater."

"Aye, aye, cap."

I was hoping the language affectation would wear off after the sails went up, because it was already getting annoying. Meanwhile, I made a beeline for the bow. When I reached the gym bag, I just stared at it for a moment. I had its consequences in mind, the illegal ones. I actually thought about kicking the bag overboard right there, in the middle of the East Basin channel. Watching it sink. Or at least float past my boat and out of my hair. That would have been the smart thing to do. But what if Pete came looking for it? What would I tell him, and how might his reaction ruin my day? Or my life?

Which was when it dawned on me that Pete might already be aboard the Carillion. In my head I went through everything that I'd done since waking that morning. There weren't a lot of places to hide on a thirty-six foot sailboat, but had I checked the forward cabin? Had I been in there at all this morning? Could Pete have slipped aboard while I was retrieving Trent? Yes, that was possible: he could be below in one of the cabins; I was sure I hadn't been in either of them since Trent and I arrived at the Carillion. Was Trent part of this?

I picked up the gym bag by its handles. It felt empty. I could tell there was something in it, but whatever it was, it didn't weigh much. I then checked the boat's position in the channel to make sure Trent wasn't about to plow us into anything, which he wasn't. Straight down the middle, like I had told him. Like he had been helming a sailboat for years. I looked back to Trent. He was now sporting a pair of wayfarer sunglasses and when he saw me looking back to him, he smiled and waved. I waved back and returned to my suspicion that Trent might have something to do with this. Which was preposterous. I scolded myself; these were two completely unrelated events. Please let them be unrelated, because my brain couldn't process any other scenario. Really, it all depended on what was in the gym bag. So I headed astern, gym bag clenched fiercely in one hand, just like Pete had done. Christ.

"How'm I doing?" asked Trent when I stepped into the cockpit.

"Awesome, skipper. What's our boat speed?"

"One point seven knots," he reported without having to look at the knot meter.

"Where's the wind coming from?" I asked. It was a trick question, intended to occupy Trent's brain for a moment. Boat speed creates a shift in wind direction. And right on cue, Trent craned his head to try to determine where it was coming from. Because I was getting the hang of his brain. Right about now he would be calculating the difference between the wind caused by the boat's motion and the real wind direction, what sailors call true wind. Which gave me enough time to slip down below with the gym bag.

I ducked into the aft cabin which is situated underneath the cockpit on this boat, so I was out of Trent's line of sight. I was pretty sure he wouldn't abandon his post. So I unzipped the gym back. Inside was a manila envelope, one of the padded types: plastic bubble wrap sandwiched in between the envelope's paper. It had been sliced open at the top, neatly, like with a knife or a razor blade. There were two thin metallic plates inside, each of which was wrapped in clear plastic, like food wrap. I pulled one of the plates out and, after studying the image etched onto the plate, realized I was looking at a reverse image of the back side of a hundred dollar bill. I pulled the other plate out from the padded pouch. It was the front side. Nice portrait of Benjamin Franklin. The plates were engraved, and instantly I knew what I had in my possession. A printing press, a little green and black ink, the right kind of paper, and I'd have as many Franklins as I could crank out.

Chapter Seven

This was incredibly serious. There was no way they were genuine. The printing plates used by the US government to print money are subject to unbelievable security. Virtually impossible for Pete the alleged gang member to have come into possession of genuine US currency printing plates. These were counterfeits. A federal crime. Dozens of years behind bars. And me being an ex-felon, the math would work out to a life sentence.

Pete had stashed them on my boat at some point. When, I couldn't quite figure out at the moment. But slung up on the foredeck of the Carillion? Like the bag was just thrown up there. From the dock of the slip. Or maybe from the water. Like he was in a hurry, or something. Or whoever it was. Like they were swimming. Which would explain why the gym bag was wet. Which reminded me that I had suspected Pete might be onboard. I quickly moved forward to the v-berth cabin. It was empty. Trent and I were the only people on this boat. I was heading back to the aft cabin when Trent called out.

"Which way do I go, captain?"

I knew what was happening. He had reached the middle of the East Basin where the Dominguez Channel intersects the Cerritos Channel. It's a big, wide open area of water in the channel that's surrounded by land scenery that all looks the same: stacks of truck-sized containers, cranes, and corrugated metal buildings. Clearly hard to know where you're going unless you've been there before; impossible to figure out where the actual ocean might be.

"What's your compass heading?" I asked as I slipped the plates back into their protective pouch.

"Looks like about two-fifteen," he said.

"Perfect!" I yelled back. "Maintain course and speed. Be there in a second." I dropped the manila envelope back into the gym bag, zipped it shut, and stuffed the bag under the cushions of the aft cabin berth. Not a genuinely secure location, but it would have to do for the moment.

I rejoined Trent in the cockpit, and quickly assessed our position in the basin in relation to other watercraft. The East Basin can get crazy crowded with five-hundred-foot container ships on some days, but this was a Saturday morning, and for the moment we were alone except for a tug two hundred yards off our forward port beam, heading away from us.

"This is the coolest thing I have ever done," Trent said through another goofy boyish grin.

"It gets better; we haven't even started sailing yet."

I did another three-sixty look around, just to be safe, and when I looked back to Trent, he was wiping his cheek with the sleeve of his windbreaker. At first I thought it was maybe the wind or a bug or something. But then I read the expression on his face, despite the sunglasses; the downturned lips, the taught jawline and neck muscles, the subtle bobbing head movement, a streak of water running down the other cheek: Trent Hayden was crying.

Christ. This was it. This was the point where the guy imploded, where the mask cracked and out came the real Trent Hayden, the psycho version, the one Perry had been talking about. Great. Counterfeit printing plates down below and a madman at the wheel.

"You alright, Trent?"

He exhaled something that started as a sob and then turned into a laugh, one of those voiceless, breathy, aspirated laughs. Then he sniffled a couple times and the goofy smile returned to accompany the laughing. After a second he composed himself.

"This is the first day off I've had in over eleven years," he said.

"Seriously?" Because at the age I had figured this guy for, eleven years ago would have put him in sixth grade.

"Exactly," he said. "The first serious day I've had off. I mean, sure, I get weekends away from the office, but they don't count because, you know, I'm still working, at home, on a solution or a piece of failed code. There's always something, on the agenda, on the horizon, whatever." Trent took a deep breath, then exhaled and said, "Everyone's always waiting on me."

Trent went quiet.

"Kinda like what Redman was talking about this morning," I said.

"You have no idea, Trippy, no idea. Do you know when this all started for me?"

I shook my head.

"Seventh grade, advanced placement program. That's a big deal in the Philadelphia public school system. An opportunity – *the* opportunity – the one that my parents and my family and my friends and my teachers were all waiting for and counting on. Counting on me. By the time I reached high school I was in some class, studying some subject, from seven in the morning until nine o'clock at night. Every day. Weekends, holidays. No summer breaks for me. Nope. I just took more classes. Advanced Physics. Calculus. Right angle trigonometry. Studied at school. Studied at home. Even the summer after I graduated from high school was spent at a STEM camp in Maryland.

"And after that? Straight off to college. MIT on a scholarship, where it was pretty much the same thing all over again. All my weekends and semester breaks were spent in the lab writing code, running code, analyzing code, analyzing other people's code, rewriting code, building builds, debugging builds, refining, rewriting, executing, implementing. I mean, I loved it, don't get me wrong. I was in my element, hanging out with people that were just as focused and infinitely smarter. That's where I met Darcy."

Trent fell silent again, and I started thinking about Darcy's IQ and what that meant to their relationship and what their children might be like. I figured it could go either way: geniuses or mutants.

"Next thing you know," continued Trent, "I'm being recruited by some high-tech engineering firm, and they're paying me more money in my first year than both my parents combined made in their lifetime. And I thought, finally. I finally made it. All this hard work is finally gonna start to pay off. Things'll slow down. I can catch my breath. Take a vacation. Maybe do some sailing." Trent laughed at this last observation.

"But no," I offered.

"Nope. Along came this little thing, a little clip of code called the Group of Eights sorting algorithm. I used to think my life was upside down. Then it got turned inside out, and I realized how good upside down was. Upside down became the good old days."

Trent went internal and quiet again. I was trying to think of something magical to say, something that would make a difference, like I was forcing it to happen, living up to my reputation. But nothing was coming. Probably had something to do with the discovery of counterfeit printing plates onboard. Plates that belonged to a gang member. Stolen from somewhere, most likely, and now in my possession. What my brain was dying to do was calculate the amount of prison time I'd get if I was caught with the plates.

I forced it to refocus on Trent Hayden, the guy at the wheel whose problems were finally manifesting. I thought about the pressure this kid must be under, to deliver, to meet the demands corporate America was thrusting down his young brilliant throat, in pursuit of profits. Redman was right. They had enslaved this genius.

Meanwhile the Carillion kept chugging along just under two knots, and was now passing under the Vincent Thomas Bridge, which is a pretty cool thing, and it looked like the monument distracted Trent. For the moment. He was staring up at its underside as we passed below. It's nothing like the Golden Gate in San Francisco, but it's still a feat of engineering, and having recently learned that Trent was basically an engineer – not a finance guy – with problems, I imagined the bridge held some significance for him.

I know, living right next to it, I should have some historical information about the bridge. Like a list of facts; its construction date, design innovations, length, height, whatever. I didn't even know who Vincent Thomas was. All I could manage to remember at that point in time was something a bit more macabre, and probably highly inappropriate, considering Trent's current state of mind. Quite appropriate, considering mine.

"Remember that movie Top Gun?" I asked.

"Are you kidding?" said Trent. "Tom Cruise, Val Kilmer. 'Talk to me, Goose'. Legendary."

"The director of that movie jumped off that bridge."

"Right," said Trent, recalling. "One of the Scott brothers. To his death. So that's the one."

"Yep."

Then Trent took off the sunglasses and looked me in the eye. "I'm not suicidal, Trippy."

"No, I didn't mean--"

"I'm beat up, worn out, and in desperate need of a little down time. But I'm not gonna jump off a fucking bridge."

I waited a respectful moment, and then said, "Well that's good. Because it'd be really hard to get you up there. From here, I mean."

I smiled.

So did Trent, and then we both laughed.

I was searching for some way to gently dissuade Trent from this line of questioning when he said, "I know you're an ex-felon."

Ah, so that was where he was going with this. It's not the first time. I was back on familiar terrain.

"That's true, but I wouldn't say it preoccupies me. That was years ago," I said.

"Oh, I know. Darcy looked you up. She's kind of protective of me."

"Naturally."

"You don't ever talk about that part of your life?"

"I do, when it's appropriate. Does it make you uncomfortable?"

"No," said Trent, rather blithely. "Just curious."

"Well I wouldn't recommend it. Above everything else, doing time's a tremendous waste of resource."

"Did the punishment fit the crime?"

"That answer depends on who you ask. I learned my lesson, that's for sure."

"So it changed you."

"Of course."

"But for the better, or worse?"

I smiled. "For the better, mostly. I do things differently now. I'm a bit more cautious."

"How so?"

Trent should have been a lawyer. "Well, for instance, I don't open up to people so quickly anymore." I looked Trent in the eye. "Especially the ones I've only known for a day."

Trent laughed. "C'mon, Trippy. I'm harmless. Besides, I feel like I've known you longer, for some reason."

"That would be the sailing," I said, and then took a sip of wine. It was only my third sip. I don't really drink anymore, especially when sailing with clients, but with this client, it seemed like the right thing to do. Besides, it was a cabernet, and the woodsy taste brought back a particularly pleasant memory.

I could sense that Trent wanted more from me, of the intimate detail variety. This was a bonding moment for him, and being now familiar with this man's penchant for intensity, I struggled to build in my mind a dialog that would not only be appropriately intense, but satisfying as well.

"I had miscalculated the consequences of my actions," I said. "In some twisted way, it had seemed like the right thing to do, at the time, and I justified it, while all along, there was that nagging voice in the back of my head telling me this was leading to nowhere good. Of course, I was high at the time, so I ignored that voice – Christ, I ignored everything – and the next thing I knew, I was handcuffed, sitting in the back of a police cruiser. The rest is a matter of public record. So I guess one of the things I learned from the whole experience is to pay more attention to that little voice in the back of your head. That, and chemical abstinence."

I looked to Trent to gauge his reaction to this uncharacteristic confession. His head was down, focused on the wine glass in his hands, of which two fingers were precisely pinching by the stem. He was gently rotating the glass, causing strands of liquid to drool down the inside, and back to the pool of wine. I never know if I've said the wrong thing, or have said too much, and always assume I've done both until I hear what the response is to my ill-spoken words.

Trent remained like this, quiet and contemplative, for a long time, to the point where I was regretting ever opening my big mouth, when he said, "Do we have reception out here?"

"You mean like for a cell phone?"

"Yeah."

"Usually, as long as we're close to the island like this."

Trent then set the wine glass down on the cockpit settee, and headed below. I heard the sound of a zipper, twice, and a moment later he reappeared at the steps leading up and out of the Carillion's saloon with a smart phone in hand. He worked the device for a second, then placed the phone to his ear.

After another pause he said in the phone, "I think I like the sound of your voice more than anything else in this world."

Which I took as a cue to give the guy some privacy, so I got up and headed forward to the pointy end of the Carillion. The last words I heard Trent say before I was out of earshot were ones reassuring the person on the phone – his wife, I had presumed – that everything was just fine. Which made me feel better. Maybe for once I had said the right thing at the right time. If that were true, I'd have to record it in the ship's log.

Less than two minutes later, Trent joined me at the ship's bow.

"My wife was right about you," he said.

"In a good way?"

Trent laughed. "Yeah, in a good way. You know she read about you in a People magazine article?"

"That's not me," I said. "People think it is, but it's not. That was somebody else."

"Right," said Trent. Like he'd never believe that. "Anyway, I know this is kind of rude, but I was wondering if we could cut this trip short and head back."

"Right now? We could, but I wouldn't advise it. This stretch of water can get a little crowded for night sailing."

"No, no. I meant tomorrow. First thing. I've got some work to do tonight."

"Work? I thought the whole point of this trip was to get away from work."

Trent smiled and put his hand on my shoulder. "You inspired me, Trippy."

"Right," I said, like I'd never believe that.

"I've been hearing that nagging little voice in the back of my head for about a week straight," he said. "I guess I can't ignore it anymore. And now I'm hearing the jingling of handcuffs."

"God forbid," I said. "Anyway, you're the skipper, skipper. We'll leave whenever you say so."

"Aye aye, captain," said Trent. And then he saluted me.

"Give it a rest," I said.

Trent smiled and headed aft, first to the cockpit, and then below into the boat's cabin.

The nagging voice.

Funny how it always seems to be the voice of the good side of the brain that gets labeled as the nag. The bad side, with its outstanding reputation – and track record – always gets the cool adjectives: tempting, alluring, seductive.

At that moment, those two sides of my brain were roiled in debate.

Something about the pros and cons of printing my own hundred-dollar bills.

Chapter Nine

I had never seen nor heard of the type of laptop Trent was using, an MSI, and although I was curious, decided not to interrupt whatever it was he was doing. It looked important. He was seated at the nav station, hunched over the computer's keyboard. There were multiple windows opened on the screen, all of them filled with short lines of text in different colors against a contrasted background color. Tech stuff, I assumed. He also had a pad of graph paper on the small table, and was working it with a mechanical pencil. I moved past him just loudly enough not to startle, but quietly enough I hoped as not to disturb.

The nav station on the Carillion is situated directly in front of the entrance to the aft cabin – the captain's cabin – which was where the gym bag and its contraband was located. There was no way I could politely slip by Trent to get into the berth without disrupting the genius at work. So I headed forward to the v-berth, which was where I usually put the guests. I climbed in to the space designed to accommodate two adults, fluffed one of the eight decorator pillows scattered about and got comfortable. I needed to think about the implications of the gym bag and its contents.

Turning them over to the police seemed like the most practical thing to do, except being an ex-felon, that whole process could go south for me in a heartbeat. And it probably wouldn't be the local cops; it would be the feds, asking hard and pointed questions that would make me squirm at the least, possibly condemn me. How did I know Pete the gang member? Had I associated with him before? Perhaps while locked up? Did I know he was transporting counterfeiting plates? Didn't I find his behavior and his unusual request for transportation suspicious? And yet I failed to report said suspicion. Why did I delay in reporting my possession of the contraband? Why did I visit Catalina Island with the contraband, and why did I bring along a computer scientist? Did I know that transporting the plates off US soil was yet another violation of federal law?

And those were the good guys asking the questions. Pete's people, on the other hand – the proverbial gang – would use a more direct approach: give us the fucking plates or we'll shoot you in the head. Which we might do anyway, depending on our mood. In fact, we have to shoot you because you've seen our faces and you know we have the plates and we can't take any chances. Even if it turns out you don't have the plates we have to kill you. And sink the boat. Burn and sink you and your boat. After we shoot you in the head. No evidence that way. Forensic evidence. Yeah, we watch CSI, too. Raised on it. One of our favorite shows.

I saw no positive outcome in any scenario. I saw only complications, and the biggest one – which was also my primary concern – was the guy seated at the nav station, Trent Hayden. If I did live through this, what would I say to Darcy? Sorry about the bullet being put through the head of the love of your life, or sorry, but your husband's been taken hostage by a local gang?

I realized I was getting worked up about events that had yet to occur. Something my court-ordered therapist from years ago called projecting. Trent and I were still safe, and so were the counterfeiting plates. I could just give them back to Pete at some point. Just hand him the gym bag and say, *Oh, by the way, found this onboard. Is it yours?* and that would be the end of it. He'd probably thank me, and we'd both be on our way. And Trent would thank me for a lovely time sailing. And his lovely wife would be happy her lovely husband wasn't dead. She'd be thankful. Everything would be lovely. Everybody would be thankful.

If only I could convince myself of this fairy tale outcome.

I've never been particularly religious, but being a recovering addict, I've worked enough twelve-step programs in my life to recognize that there was nothing I could do at the moment about this predicament, and worrying about it wouldn't help. I recalled some clever saying from one of the many programs that went something like putting one foot in front of the other and eventually arriving somewhere, presumably a place better than where I was at the moment. That worked for me, albeit weakly, and after wrestling with a variety of prospective mental demons in the guise of prison jumpsuits, gang signs, and bullet wounds, I fell asleep to the sound of Trent clacking away at his laptop keyboard.

* * *

Seven hours of sleep did my conscience wonders, and I woke up believing that getting the plates back to their original owner was the only path of action capable of fulfilling that fairy tale outcome. I would attempt to trace Pete through the referral client he had mentioned. No one had to die in the process.

I'm the type of person who needs something hot and liquid right after sleep, preferably coffee, otherwise I'm useless for about forty minutes. And grumpy. So I made my way to the ship's galley and got the coffee started. Trent was still seated at the nav station focused on his laptop, and also on the phone. He was telling someone to recompile something. I headed up to the cockpit and looked around. It was another gray morning, but being anchored in a quiet bay on a still sea makes everything look beautiful, even in overcast. The hills surrounding Catalina Harbor are rugged and rolling, painted in field grass the color of straw and brief bursts of stubborn weathered green that abruptly ends in ocean-eroded sandy brown and gray cliffs. And just as abruptly, land meets a sea that is a brighter shade of blue here, than along the mainland. It is both serene and dramatic, and possesses its very own magic of the alluring variety. I would live here if I could afford it.

The Carillion was firm on its mooring can, which is how boats anchor in this particular harbor. Instead of dropping an actual anchor, you tie the boat up to floating mooring points that themselves are anchored to the bottom via steel cable. Anchoring is neat and orderly this way, and allows for more boats to squeeze into one place, which happens a lot during the summer months. This weekend however, it was early enough in May that the Carillion pretty much had the place to herself, which is why I prefer this part of Catalina. I counted six other boats in the entire harbor; there was room for maybe fifty more.

When I returned below, Trent was off the phone, and while I poured coffee for the both of us, he began talking about the previous night's work, and in so doing, revealed the real reason for the meltdown. Honestly, I wasn't fully awake, but I got the gist that his employers were considering selling the company, and the real problem was who the prospective buyer might be. Because of the new algorithm – a term I still wasn't comfortable using because I didn't know exactly what it meant – the company Trent worked for had become hot property overnight in a variety of markets. Major players in business, finance, and tech industries were all eager to gobble up Sandfall Paradigm. Trent had urged management to stay within the tech sector, but apparently greed had played its part, naturally, and Trent did not approve of the direction the company was leaning. Which was when the tantrum came into play. It wasn't just Trent refusing to show up for work; it was the threat he would abandon work on the algorithm, or worse, sabotage it.

Now Trent was admitting, to me at least, that it was a childish move. He had spent the night, dividing his time between the laptop and the cellphone, in an attempt to repair the damage he had done over the past week, and now, this morning, was feeling better about the whole situation. And himself. Of course he was convinced I had had something to do with all of this. He used the word catalyst more than once.

I've seen this so many times before it no longer fazes me. You happen to be standing next to someone seated at a slot machine when they win the jackpot and suddenly you're their lucky charm, their magic, their catalyst. Trent, all on his own, would have come to this stunning internal revelation of his eventually; it just happened to occur while aboard the Carillon, and since I was the only human within reach, I was getting all the credit. I deflected the compliment back to where it belonged – on him – and then asked what time he thought we should head back to the mainland. He slapped his laptop shut, jumped up to attention, saluted me, and jubilantly reported he was ready when I was, captain.

Jesus Christ.

I poured myself another cup of coffee and asked him if he wanted anything to eat before we got underway. He pointed to an empty bowl and spoon that I hadn't noticed when making the coffee, then apologized for getting into the ship's stores without checking with me first. He had found the cereal and the milk about four o'clock this morning, and the bad news was we were out of milk. There was still half a box of Cocoa Krispies left. If only all of my clients were this self-sufficient. I grabbed a couple of three-month-old granola bars out of a plastic bin, and subsequently discovered stale granola bars taste better when dunked in fresh black coffee.

*   *   *

The winds were light and variable as we rounded the island's west end and headed back to San Pedro, so we motor-sailed, which is exactly what it sounds like: the sails are up but the engine does most of the work. With a northeast heading and a fairly flat sea we were making just under six knots, which would put us in San Pedro sometime in the midafternoon. Not surprisingly, Trent was in complete control of the ship; he maintained a steady course while I did some housework down below. Some people shy away from being below deck while underway, but I like listening to the engine, if for no other reason than being able to hear when something goes wrong. Boats are unique in that respect; there aren't a lot of floating repair shops between the mainland and the island, and in my experience, the sooner you can detect a problem, the easier, faster, and less expensive it is to fix. But on this particular morning, she was happily humming away at a steady twenty-three hundred RPMs, which to a motoring sailor is the song of heaven.

Trent spent most of the return trip chasing the wind, which is natural. At least twice he asked if we could alter course because he thought he saw some puffs to our right or left. I said that was up to him, whether he could afford the time. But it only took one failed attempt before Trent recognized the futility of his efforts, and decided to stick to the direct bearing. Welcome to sailing, I said to him. Honestly, the fact that he got to lean the boat over in moderate winds on the way to the island was more than most clients got, but I didn't tell him that, and thus his expectations were predictably high. Not all sailing was as good as we had it the day before, but I was fairly sure Trent would figure that out at some point all on his own. Maybe not on this trip, but someday.

San Pedro sits on the edge of the Los Angeles Harbor, which is part of a southern-facing crescent-shaped indentation in the land that stretches for ten-miles along the coast of Southern California and includes Long Beach Bay, Alamitos Bay, and probably a couple other bays that I'm not aware of. It all starts with a jut of land called Point Fermin and runs due east to Seal Beach. Almost all ten of those ocean miles are protected by a seawall called the San Pedro breakwater. On a clear day, you can see it from about a mile out, and Trent got excited when he spotted it, mostly because it was a validation of his helmsman skills.

Prior to the sighting of the seawall, Trent had been going on about his wife, Darcy, whom I learned spent most of her time at MIT in the Brain and Cognitive Sciences department. Which caused me to wonder why the couple hadn't handled Trent's mini-breakdown internally. You know, if you're married to some sort of shrink, why look elsewhere? And then I started thinking maybe that was Darcy's plan from the beginning. Maybe Trent needed something completely different, and Darcy knew that, which was why she took the trouble to track me down. Granted, it was speculation on my part, and having two failed marriages on my record, poorly-founded speculation at that.

Nonetheless, the timing was perfect when Trent spotted the seawall, because it changed the subject and stopped me from trying to psychoanalyze the Haydens. It was also a teaching moment, so with the Carillion on autopilot, I invited Trent below to show him what the breakwater looked like on the San Pedro nautical chart. It would only take a minute, I reckoned, and having already scanned the horizon to determine there was no traffic in our vicinity, I felt safe in leaving the helm on autopilot. Of course, I had forgotten this was some genius level engineer looking at the chart, so after about three minutes of Trent memorizing the plotted locations of buoy markers, shipping channels and light beacons in the Los Angeles harbor, I reminded him that no one was at the wheel. He corrected me: there was a computer at the wheel, and statistically speaking, computers commit far less errors than humans.

Statistically speaking.

We bounced back topside, and this time I let Trent check for traffic. It was all clear, he reported, except for a speck of a craft about a thousand yards behind us approaching on our port side. I reassured Trent this was common: just another vessel heading back to San Pedro, as we were. Then I showed him how to use the approaching vessel's angle relative to the Carillion's position to determine if the paths of the two crafts would intersect. As long as that angle didn't stay the same, the two boats would not collide.

But the angle stayed the same.

We were on a collision course.

Chapter Ten

I took a better look for myself, and sure enough, the approaching vessel looked as though it was headed right for us and at a decent rate of speed. It probably wasn't aiming for us, but when you're only managing five knots speed, it tends to feel like it. The other boat was riding low in the water and was kicking up a sizeable white water tail and long wake. I guessed it was an offshore powerboat, something over twenty feet in length. If my guess was correct, it was a type of boat that was designed for speed on the ocean, like over fifty miles an hour no problem. There are a few offshore racing clubs out of Long Beach, so it wasn't too surprising to see something like this, especially on a Sunday morning. Boats capable of that level of speed tend to see boats like ours as stationary objects. They'd probably blow past us with a couple hundred feet to spare, and I said that to Trent. Besides, I told him, there was still enough time to maneuver, should the need arise.

The approaching vessel was now directly on our stern, maybe two hundred yards behind, and still bearing down on us at what looked like well over thirty knots. I was growing concerned. I instructed Trent to turn ninety degrees to port and throttle the engine up to twenty-six hundred RPMs. Almost all boats have autopilots these days, and a technologically advanced powerboat such as the one on our tail might have a GPS-linked autopilot, which meant the vessel would pursue a straight line course with terminator accuracy and without human intervention. I'd heard stories of GPS-guided boats ramming other boats or plowing into shore or the seawall at breakneck speed because the pilot had set the GPS and autopilot, and then headed below deck to join the party. Which might have been the case here, which was why I had Trent make the course alteration. We were now traveling perpendicular to the approaching vessel's path of travel. If their course corrected, then I would assume the boat was targeting us.

Its course corrected. She was now heading for our broadside.

If the pilot of that vessel intended on ramming us, there wasn't much we could do aboard the Carillion. Maybe abandon ship by jumping into the water, but there was no telling how the impact might happen. Neither Trent nor I were wearing life vests; they were resting uselessly on a seat cushion in the cabin below.

"Kill the power, put her into neutral," I said to Trent. I then grabbed hold of the mainsheet, unwrapped it from its winch, and did the same for the jib sheet, putting both sails in a lazy flap in the light wind. I heard the engine revs drop to idle, confirming Trent had de-powered the boat, so I jumped into the cabin and grabbed the life preservers.

Trent said, "They're gonna hit us."

"Looks like it. Here," I said as I handed him a vest, "Put this on and get ready to jump."

"Are they crazy?" asked Trent as he fumbled with the plastic clips of the life vest.

"Probably drunk."

The other boat was now close enough that I could see I was wrong about her size. She was well over thirty feet, a racing catamaran design: split hulls painted in gradient purple and yellow that tapered to twin bows of knobby blunted points. Probably Kevlar construction. If she hit us at her current speed the powerboat would literally pierce our hull, causing the Carillion to explode into ripped and frayed pieces of fiberglass. If there was any good news, it was that I could see people in the cockpit, three of them, all with black hair being buffeted by the wind. And sunglasses. The wraparound kind.

"Get ready," I said to Trent, and we both took hold of a stanchion on the cockpit's starboard side of the Carillion. "Jump as far away as you can and towards the stern."

Less than a hundred feet from impact, I heard the boat's power cut off as she veered to the right of the Carillion. Again, I realized I was wrong about her length. Had to be close to fifty feet. The vessel had the name 'TomCat' splashed on her side in a stylized mixture of the same yellow and purple. Open cockpit, two rows of seats, three males in front, two in the row behind, also male. Four of the five heads in the boat, all wearing what looked like identical wraparound sunglasses, swiveled on us as they coasted past us no more than ten feet away.

For some reason I focused on the guy who wasn't wearing matching sunglasses and whose head wasn't tracking us. He was in the front row, seated between the pilot and the passenger. Then I discovered why. He was slumped forward, his face and hair coated in what looked like coagulated blood.

"You guys alright?" I shouted as they floated ahead of us, still decelerating from the speed build up.

No response, but I heard the engine idle drop and the transmission clunk as it went into gear.

She began circling us, slowly, the guy at the wheel bringing the TomCat closer to the Carillion on each pass.

"What's going on?" I asked of the other vessel. Do you require assistance?" Trent and I were now standing square in the cockpit, maintaining our balance as the Carillion reacted to the combination of a gentle ocean swell and the wake from the other boat.

"What the fuck is this, Trippy?" said Trent in a tense and hushed tone. He sounded like I felt: scared.

"Just be cool. See what they want."

Of course I had a really good idea what the fuck this was, and it had to do with the counterfeit plates. That was the only explanation. In my twenty-five years of sailing, nothing like this had ever happened to me. Had to be Pete and his alleged gang. Except these guys didn't look like Hispanic gang members. It was hard to tell with the sunglasses, but if I had to guess, I'd say they were Asian. It was the cut, color and texture of their hair, their complexion, and the line of their jaws. The only one who looked different was the motionless guy with the bloody head, who was also the only one wearing a life preserver.

On their third rotation around the Carillion, the pilot aligned the TomCat so she was coming up alongside our port side. And that's when Trent and I both saw the weapons.

"Jesus Christ," said Trent.

"Just be cool, be cool."

They looked like automatic machine pistols, the short stubby kind where the ammo clip extended straight down, and was longer than the gun barrel. Both men in the back were armed, as was the guy seated in the front passenger spot, to the right of the bloody lifeless man. This was the one who said something to the others. It wasn't a language I recognized except that it added to my suspicion that they might be Asian. The two in back stepped out of the cockpit seats and up onto the rear deck of the boat. They were wearing dark suits and open collar white shirts, which made no sense to me. Nobody dresses like that to go boating. Except maybe bad guys in a B movie. They kept their weapons low and trained on us. The pilot idled the TomCat's engine and the powerboat settled inches from the Carillion.

The two standing on the powerboat's deck were getting ready to jump onboard the Carillion when the pilot said something in that same foreign language and pointed ahead and to the right, towards the bow of the Carillion. Everyone's head turned toward the direction the pilot was pointing except mine. I was keeping my eye on the weapons. The guy in the passenger seat responded with something that sounded like an order, barked out quickly and with authority. That changed everything. The two men standing instantly jumped down into the cockpit and back into their seats just as the pilot slammed the throttle forward, causing the offshore racer's bow to lurch up as at least two racing propellers below the split hulls dug deeply into the water, thrusting the boat forward. The arched bow dipped to the left as the driver pivoted the wheel and cut away from the Carillion at a sharp angle. A couple seconds later they were hundreds of yards away from us.

I felt safe enough to look in the direction the pilot had pointed. It was a Coast Guard response boat with its tell-tale orange and white colorings and a red-painted underhull, heading towards us at what looked like full throttle. Trent was looking, too.

"That would be the good guys", I said. "Coast Guard."

"Are you kidding me?" exclaimed Trent. He was smiling, that same goofy, boyish grin. Then he looked at me. "You are amazing!"

"What?"

"Pirates! You arranged for pirates to attack our ship! That was so awesome! They were gonna board us and probably make us walk the plank or something! Like right out of a movie! What kind of boat was that? Can you get me a ride on that thing? Did you see how fast it took off!? Best day ever!"

I was dumbfounded for a second before I realized this was an opportunity – the golden kind – presenting itself to me. Having Trent think this was all staged was the perfect excuse. Because just two seconds ago, I was planning on telling my new best friend geek that there were counterfeit printing plates onboard, and that was probably the reason why the guys in the superboat with guns had just about ended our lives. Because it was the only explanation that made any sense. To me, at least.

Except for the one that Trent had just come up with: that I had dreamt all this up just to impress the client.

I tried to put on a sad face. "How'd you figure it out so quickly?"

And of course the engineer analyst programmer geek – who didn't really have any problems, it turns out – had it all figured out. It was the timing, he said, almost back to port – the end of a perfect sailing adventure – and the costumes and the foreign language and that awesome boat and the way they almost rammed us but didn't because they were like totally pro drivers, and those awesome looking machines guns – machine guns on the open seas!! – it was just too perfect, he said. *Straight out of a movie!* he repeated. *Awesome!* he repeated. *Nobody has that much adventure packed into such a tiny amount of time, unless it was planned!*

Like it was part of the package. The thought crossed my mind that I might even be able to pass off the counterfeit plates stashed below as part of the act, but with the Coast Guard rapidly approaching, decided against it. Instead, I gave Trent all the credit for seeing through my ruse. Most clients are completely fooled, I said, but I forgot who I was dealing with. I then complimented him on how he had kept his cool.

Trent was beaming proud. So with one problem solved, I had another one rapidly approaching at about thirty knots. There was no doubt the Coast Guard vessel was heading right for us. Which meant they would most likely board us. Which meant they would search and find the plates. So that would be two problems. First, how do I keep Trent convinced this was an act, and second, how do I handle the Coast Guard. Alright, back to just one problem: how to handle the Coast Guard. Because once they found the counterfeit plates, there would be no point in continuing the pretense that had so satisfied my effervescing client.

The response boat had slowed about a hundred feet from our location, and was preparing to come alongside the

Carillion. A voice amplified by loudspeaker announced its arrival.

"Skipper of the vessel, heave to and prepare to be boarded!"

The sails were already eased so I held one hand high in the air and gave the Coast Guard vessel the thumbs up.

"This is so cool!" said Trent.

"Look. Let me do all the talking. Pirate gags don't go over well with these guys, so let me handle this."

"Aye aye, captain!" Trent could barely contain his excitement.

Jesus Christ.

I quickly kicked fenders over the side of the Carillion just as the forty-foot response boat bounced up against us. In less than a second three armed Guardsman dressed in dark blue overalls boarded the Carillion. They had machine guns, too, and I thought how wonderful it was to live in a country where everyone can brandish their own automatic weapons. One of the boarders reached up to the boom and pushed it alee, or away from the wind, off the boat's centerline, and out of their way. The other marine trooper began an immediate inspection of the Carillion. That left Trent and myself with the third Guardsman, the guy in charge, evidently, who gave us both a good look over.

"Are you the skipper?" he said to me.

"Yes, sir."

"What the hell was that all about?"

So I told him the absolute truth. Except for the machine guns part. We thought we were going to be rammed, had prepared to abandon ship, but they didn't, and as they got closer, realized that one of their crew – not the pilot – appeared to be injured so we offered to render assistance, but there was a language barrier so they took off just as fast as they had arrived.

And that was all we knew. Because I was certain if I mentioned the guns, we'd be hauled in and interviewed and documented and photographed and background checked, and it wouldn't take the feds long to learn that I was a felon, and by then they'd have found the counterfeit plates, and that would be the end of a lot of things. I knew better than to go there. Even if it meant lying.

There were now two Guardsmen down in the Carillion's cabin. I couldn't see what they were doing. I wanted to know where they were searching, what they had found, but thought it best to maintain eye contact with the one asking questions. Any other behavior on my part might look suspicious. And cops, whether on land or at sea or in the air, were naturally suspicious. I didn't need to help them along.

He was asking me what sort of injury I had observed. I explained the appearance of blood on the man's head. Which was when Trent chimed in, telling the officer that his whole head was drenched in blood.

Then the officer turned to Trent and did me a huge favor. He said, "Right now I'm talking with the skipper of the vessel, sir. I ask that you please wait."

Trent shrunk back a step and shoved his hands in his pockets. I love the Coast Guard. So professional. Procedural.

Just then one of the Guardsmen from below stepped back into the cockpit. He had something in his hand, but it looked white, not the yellow of a padded manila envelope or the green of a gym bag. It was the boat's paperwork and registration, along with my wallet. He also had the folded pink receipt from the last time I was inspected by the Coast Guard, about four months ago. I keep all that stuff in the nav station table storage for easy access, presumably for situations just like this. The Guardsman handed the paperwork and wallet to the one asking the questions who looked it over, then looked back at me.

"You Frank Deason?"

"Yes sir. My license should be in the wallet."

from the atmosphere and trapping it in those crystals. And then that dirty salt begins to chew and eat and gnaw and grind. At everything. All the time. Day and night. Left unabated, it'll destroy everything in its path. Probably not in my lifetime, but there's still that chance, and I didn't want that happening to the Carillon. Because destruction like that rarely occurs while she's sitting in the slip. It's like life in that respect: failure always strikes at the most inconvenient time.

Amen.

So I fetched the garden hose out of the storage bin at the head of the dock slip and began the ritual of hosing the boat down with fresh water in the hopes of preventing failure. It's a mindless activity really, like watering a lawn I'd imagine, and that gave my brain time to ponder my predicament.

It was too much of a coincidence that both the visitors at sea courtesy the offshore powerboat and the ones on dry land appeared to be Asian. But I didn't get the connection. The visiting gang members made more sense; they were looking for the printing plates that were in Pete's possession. They obviously knew where Pete had met his fate. And if they were privy to the fact that Pete had hitched a ride with me a couple days ago, the Carillion was a likely place to begin looking.

I know, I was making a boatload of assumptions, but I didn't have much else to work with. So I told my brain to take a step back and to think about what I did know, what the facts were. It was pretty obvious. Fact Number One was that hundred dollar bill counterfeit printing plates were a hot commodity. Anybody would love to get their hands on them. Hell, if I had the means of production, I'd pump out a couple thousand and go buy myself one of those Teslas. And new sails. And put the change in my pocket. But I didn't have a printing press. Or the paper. Or the ink. Oddly enough, the Carillion wasn't set up to print money. But there had to be people that were set up for that. Governments, and other organizations. Criminal organizations, like Pete's gang. How had Pete gotten his hands on them? Are gangs in the business of designing and producing counterfeit printing plates? Do they have the production capabilities? How difficult would that be?

I was back to assuming, and it dawned on me that my brain loves to assume. Maybe all brains do, but mine seems to prefer it. Or worse, enjoys it. But the assumption that Pete had stolen the printing plates rather than designing and producing them himself seemed like a safe one. It bordered on being a fact.

Then I got the connection. I was standing in the Carillion's cockpit, spraying it down with the garden hose, watching the water collect and drain out the scuppers in the sole of the boat, when a whole bunch of my assumptions lined up, one connecting to another with a kind of plausible logic that can make assumptions look exactly like facts. Pete had stolen the plates, and the Asians were the ones he had stolen them from. An Asian gang? Couldn't be a government. What Asian government would have any interest in printing counterfeit American dollars?

And that question triggered a memory from prison. Not one of roll call and jumpsuits or burpies on the yard in triple digit heat. It was a lesson in economics, courtesy the New York Times. Some knucklehead housed in the same dormitory as me had managed to get himself a free month's subscription to the Times just by writing a letter to the newspaper's subscription desk. And as surprising as it may seem, newspapers are considered hot property on the inside. So I got in line, which meant after everyone else had read the paper, snatched articles from it, folded it, shuffled it, bunched it, torn it, burned holes in it, written on it, completed the crossword puzzle in it and put it on top of a locker that was designated as the depository for free reading material, I got my hands on it.

Which was where I learned about inflation, and how printing too much currency can lead to it. Accordingly, because of inflation's economic impact on nations, lots of

Chapter Fourteen

What the fuck did he just say? said the bad side of my brain, who saw this purely as an opportunity to reintroduce its side of the argument.

I was in deep shit. The good side was nowhere to be found. I became acutely aware of my body movement, my facial reactions, the sudden involuntary twitching of my fingers. I told myself to take a really deep breath, which I couldn't, because that would have been a body movement.

"Excuse me? Did you say Pete?" I was sure it sounded weak, but it was the best I could manage. I wanted it to feel like they had mentioned a name I should know, but didn't, or couldn't recall at the time. The young couple, so full of promise and hope and love, but not really, were both being so casual about this, relaxed, at home on my boat, like we were all good friends, talking about the weather, or the practicality of glassware on a sailboat.

Come on, Trippy!" said Doug. I had told them my name was Frank. Never mentioned the nickname. "You were with him Friday," he said, like everybody knew this, common knowledge.

"Funny, you don't look like you worked with Pete," I said.

Doug and Nell shared a look.

Nell looked back to me and said, "You were one of the last people to see him."

"But not the very last," I said. "You guys cops?"

"Let's assume he has them," Nell said. "Because then we can talk about it and maybe save everybody a lot of time."

It took me a second to realize that even though she was looking straight at me, she was talking to Doug.

"This whole thing was your idea, anyway," said Doug. Also not talking to me.

"He knows what they are, but he hasn't a clue what to do with them," said Nell.

Doug said, "Can't turn them in to the cops because he's an ex-con. Doesn't want to implicate himself."

"And he can't give them back to Pete because Pete's dead," said Nell. "But I bet that's what he wishes he could do."

"But if he gives them back to Pete's people, we're right back where we started," said Doug. "In fact, that would end it. We'd have to start all over."

The casual conversation between good friends. Nell was leaned back in the saloon seats, legs crossed over, her arms draped over the back of the bench seat, one hand still holding the plastic cup with the German wine. Doug was now standing in the galley playing with the lever that pumped salt water into the galley sink.

"Why don't I just give them back to you?" I said.

Nell smiled, looked to Doug and said, "Winner, winner!" She held a hand up for Doug to high-five, which he did.

"How do you do that?" said Doug to Nell. "That's like the third time you've guessed and been right."

"Because no one else had them. The only other place they could be is here. Or at the bottom of the ocean, and I don't think Pete would let that happen," said Nell. "If they weren't here, they weren't anywhere."

"Chicken dinner," said Doug.

Oddly, I found myself thinking how all of this – my current dilemma of two strangers, who I thought were really nice people, who wanted to learn more about sailing, who given me a three hour window. I would have been gone before they even realized I might be gone. But we both know how that would have ended. People like Doug and Nell – and whoever their people were – had the capability of preventing total strangers from making their flight just by causing car accidents. At a moment's notice. Not like they carefully planned it out and staged it, but by sending a text message. At least that's how I figured it all went down. Nell had texted one of her people, and less than ten minutes later, Trent and Darcy were missing their flight back home.

So running would have bought me some time, but that was about it. And more time only complicated matters. Because they would take Trent and Darcy to a black site or a safe house or a holding cell and waterboard them. Not because torture would reveal to people like Doug and Nell where I was, but because that's what people like Doug and Nell did. They waterboarded first and then asked questions. I wasn't interested in acquiring more time, or getting the Haydens waterboarded; I wanted this whole thing to be over. Fast. And the way Doug and Nell had pitched it, this current path seemed to be the shortest distance between two points. That, and the fact that there were no other points or paths to consider.

It was now after eleven on a Sunday night, and I found myself thanking god no one else was in the parking lot. Like Redman. Because he would ask what I was doing, and that would have required lying. Not that I don't lie, but that kind of goes against that whole Your Life Matters thing. Redman's life matters. Trent's and Darcy's lives matter.

I felt stupid when Doug and Nell arrived in a brand new, shiny black Mercedes S500 with dealer plates. An AMG Mercedes. Yep, the very same one. Under my nose. At least it looked identical. It pulled up right in front of me and the driver's tinted window slid down to reveal Doug behind the wheel. Nell smiled and waved to me from the passenger seat. Like cousins picking you up for a family reunion.

I got in the back seat, and Nell said, "Where are the plates?"

"On the boat," I said.

Doug had driven about a hundred feet from where they had picked me up when he slammed on the brakes. "What the fuck?"

"No, Trippy," said Nell.

"Go get 'em," said Doug.

"What, the plates?"

"Uh, yeah," said Nell. Indignant. Impatient. Like I should know better.

"Now," said Doug. He started backing the Mercedes up. Like he was upset. He stopped the car directly across from the gate.

I got out and closed the door.

DOUG AND NELL

Inside the Mercedes, Doug and Nell high-fived each other.

"You think we're being too hard on him?" asked Nell.

"Maybe," said Doug. But I haven't had this much fun in a long time."

"Me neither."

Nell's cell phone rang.

"Hello? Hi Darcy!" Nell smiled and glanced at Doug as she listened. "Oh please, it was clearly my brother's fault. He's a horrible driver! I am so sorry you two missed your flight. Are you kidding? Buying you guys dinner was the least we could do. And we've arranged for a car to take you to the airport. Well, you're welcome. I'm just really grateful you've been so understanding about all of this. It's such an embarrassment."

Nell winked at Doug while she listened. "It was? I'm glad you both enjoyed it. They say it's one of the best restaurants in town. Well it was our pleasure. Listen, you keep my number and the next time you two are in Los Angeles I promise we'll get together, even if it's only for a cup of coffee. Okay. You, too. Safe flight! Bye."

Nell disconnected the call.

Doug said, "Why is he so important?"

"Bill likes the company he works for. Sandfall something or other."

"Like an investment?"

"Maybe. All I know is they're in tech, and he's supposedly some sort of whiz."

"Oh." Doug looked out the tinted window. "Here he comes. Lucky for you she didn't call when he was in the car."

"That gives me an idea. Want to have some more fun with him?"

Doug looked to Nell and smiled. "You already know the answer to that."

They high-fived.

Nell put the cellphone to her ear and waited.

Chapter Seventeen

I had run from the gate to the boat, jumped onboard, fumbled with the lock on the cabin hatch, went below, pulled the padded envelope containing the plates out of the gym bag from under the aft cabin bed cushion, put it in the back pocket of my jeans, and was running back up the floating dock before realizing what I was doing: rushing on their account. The same people who wanted to shoot me because it fulfilled their agenda, whatever that was. It was ridiculous. I was kowtowing, and that irritated me. They should have been more specific about bringing the plates. So I stopped rushing. This was their mistake, and they could wait. I settled into a casual walk, a stroll even, as I pushed through the gate leading to the parking lot.

I hate it when people pull my strings.

As I opened the Mercedes' rear door, I heard Nell saying, "I don't give a shit if you have to peel their fingernails off one by one!"

She was on the phone, and sounding angry. She took notice as I entered the car and her tone softened. "Just find out what they know." She jabbed at the screen of the phone, dropped it into her lap, then looked up to the ceiling of the car for a moment. "Jesus Christ."

Doug said, "They're innocents, Nell."

Nell flashed an angry look to Doug. "I don't give a shit. They're expendable." She turned to look out her window. "All I care about are those goddamned plates."

She then looked back at me and smiled insincerely. "We good to go now?"

I nodded, and offered her the manila envelope. "I don't fucking want 'em," she said, then turned around to face forward.

It was awkwardly quiet as Doug put the car into gear and headed out of the marina parking lot. I had no idea who they were talking about – the innocents – but my brain couldn't help but think it was the Haydens. Convinced it was them. They don't still pull people's fingernails off, do they? That was just an expression people like Doug and Nell use, right?

Jesus Christ.

No, that would be too messy. Politically speaking, at the very least. But there were other things they could do. Other forms of torture, more subtle, less effective, more damaging, and longer lasting. And how much of it would be traced back to me? How good were these people at doing what they do and making it look like someone else had done it?

Like an ex-felon.

Maybe they were talking about someone else, another kidnapped couple.

We drove north on Henry Ford Avenue out of the marina parking lot, made a right on Anaheim Street, and ended up using Ocean Boulevard to cross over the Los Angeles River. Like we were going into downtown Long Beach. Which we were, to a hotel called the Pike. It's part of the Hyatt chain, and probably costs north of three hundred dollars a night. Underground parking with direct elevator access to the floor of your room.

Which turned out to be a suite. Over five hundred well-appointed square feet with a separate sitting area that looked out to the ocean. A couple of couches, breakfast table, a writing desk. Two queen sized beds made up with immaculate precision in crisp, bright white linen with a thread count high enough to be a zip code. Decorator throw pillows perfectly positioned about the suite. Abstract art the size of a tumbling mat on the walls. So this was what five hundred a night looked like.

Nell seemed to be in a better mood once we were in the room. All I could think about was Trent and Darcy Hayden. And their fingernails. Lack thereof, and how all of this was on account of me. I felt like shit.

"I don't care how bad your day is," Nell said, "you come home to this, you feel better about your life."

My brain was disagreeing with her. She headed straight to the minibar and opened it.

"Want anything to drink, Trippy?"

I said no, but she threw me a Pellegrino sparkling water in a tall thin aluminum can anyway. Flavored. Mandarin Raspberry, or something. Meanwhile, Doug had grabbed a couple of black duffel bags I hadn't seen when we had entered the room and put them on the bed. He unzipped them both and began searching them. There were several large packets that were tightly wrapped in what looked like shrink-wrapped plastic. He examined each packet carefully before finding the one he was interested in, and threw the others back in one of the duffel bags. Even after tearing away the plastic wrap, it still looked shiny. And dark. Some sort of garment, stiff and flat, folded down its length. When Doug unfolded it and held it up, it reminded me of the top half of a wet suit: sleek and sleeveless with a short waist. Had to be the vest they had referred to. From the Chicago thing. The zipper was in the back.

Doug looked at me, then back to the vest. "Yeah, it'll fit," he said. "Take your shirt off and come here."

I am somewhere between in shape and flabby fat. Like the middle of that somewhere, and I realized I had not been shirtless in front of strangers since prison, which was a long time ago. Oddly, I had aged since then. So I was just a little self-conscious as I shrugged out of my sweatshirt. There was a mirror on the wall over a credenza, and I saw my reflection, shirtless and a pair of jeans with a folded manila envelope sticking out of a back pocket. I sucked my gut in just as I noticed Nell checking me out. She was leaning against the writing desk drinking a canned Pellegrino just like mine, and was smiling, but I wasn't sure if it was because she was enjoying my embarrassment, or because she liked what she saw.

Doug stepped in front of me. "Arms out front," he said. He slipped the vest through and over my arms and draped it around my shoulders. It was about half an inch thick, made out of a fabric that reminded me of something between plastic and linoleum. It felt cold against my skin. Doug stepped behind me and pulled at the bottom corners of the garment.

"Suck your gut in," he said, which made Nell laugh.

I already was sucking my gut in, but I pulled my stomach and chest in even tighter and felt Doug's touch as he found and seated the zipper's catch. He zipped me up.

I could barely breathe.

Doug stepped back in front of me to admire his work. He smiled. "Perfect."

"Will it work?" I asked, my voice sounding constricted.

"What, you mean stop a bullet?" said Doug. "You bet it will. Two layers of laminated Kevlar and carbon fiber with a honeycomb layer of absorption gel in between. Blood red, by the way. So when the bullet first impacts the vest, it penetrates the initial layer which releases the gel to simulate a hit. Make it look like you got shot. The last layer is what's gonna save your life."

"What's it gonna feel like, getting shot?" I gasped.

"Like a sledgehammer to the chest." Doug then punched me in the solar plexus, without warning, hard enough to send me back two steps. "Probably lift you off your feet."

I had felt the impact, but not the punch, if that makes any sense, and Doug explained how it's all about transferring and distributing something called the bullet's penetration velocity so that it doesn't end up as a single focused force.

"It looks good on him," said Nell. "You should wear it all the time, Trippy."

Doug stopped what he was doing and looked sideways at Nell.

"Why do you always end up fucking the marks?" said Doug. "Excuse me, *falling* for them."

"I'm not going to fuck him. I'm just saying it looks good. Not hard to fall for him, though."

So now I was a mark. Doug shook his head, then bent over and began checking the fit of the vest at my waist by squeezing my love handles with his hands. Nell was looking at me the way she had before: like she wanted to cook me. Had to be cooking, because I refused to believe an attractive woman ten years my younger would be thinking dirty thoughts about me. Doug looked up to me and whispered. "Don't be surprised if she makes a pass at you."

"Pretty sure not much is going to surprise me at this point."

"That's the spirit." Doug stood up. "Alright, let's go over this."

Doug stepped over to a small round table that was pushed up against the false balcony looking out to the ocean. I joined him, and as Nell did the same, she put one arm around my waist. I looked at her, surprised after all. She stared straight into my eyes, you know, the way women do when they're coming on to you, that dead straight stare that is meant to advertise their intentions. Or maybe their desires, but in any case I had seen that look in a bunch of movies just before the love scene.

She had straight dark hair that ended at her shoulders. It was parted slightly off center, and ever since we'd met – if you can call it that – I had noticed she would occasionally brush it back with a hand to keep it from falling across her face. Or hook it behind an ear. Or toss her head to swing the strands away from her eyes. Those eyes were very dark, but had just enough flecking of honey-colored gold in them that I could tell the pupils from the iris. Her face was delicately symmetrical and was freckled, lightly enough that I hadn't noticed them until just now, which was understandable, considering her face was less than a foot from mine. At that moment, her lips parted ever so slightly, just enough to reveal a single glistening tip of a brilliant white --

Doug cleared his throat. I looked to him. He, too, was staring right at me.

Different intent.

"What did I just tell you? Not two minutes ago, right over there." He thrust a finger towards the middle of the room.

"Come on, Trippy, focus," said Nell. She had dropped her arm from my waist.

"Me?!" Like I was the distraction.

Jesus Christ.

Doug pulled a black-handled folding Buck knife out of one pocket and put it on the table. "This is you on your boat," he said. "Make sure you're in the cockpit when you make the transaction. You go below we won't have the shot."

Doug pulled an ammo clip out of his back pocket and put it on the table. It was about five inches long and loaded with fat stubby bullets that were brassy gold with dull silver tips. "This is us on our boat." He looked to me and waited until he was sure I was paying attention. "Five hundred yards, Trippy. No more than five hundred yards, or there's no guarantee on placement of the shot. The closer the better," he said.

"Wait a minute," I said. "You're going to shoot me on my boat while standing on another boat? At five hundred yards?"

"We're gonna try," said Nell.

Chapter Eighteen

"Don't worry, I got a guy that can make the shot blindfolded."

Doug had said that, and weirdly, it made sense coming from him, like that was the kind of thing these people did in their spare time, you know, when they're not peeling fingernails off innocents. *Let's see if you can hit the target with your eyes closed. Yuck Yuck Yuck.*

Which was when my brain went to a different place, the *oh well, it's raining on our picnic* place, the *it is what it is* place. Trent's and Darcy's lives were at stake, or at least the quality of those lives was, and that was on me. Which meant it was up to me to put things right. Your Life Matters. My responsibility.

Even if that meant dying.

Because I had worked it all out in my head. The goal was to get the counterfeit plates into the hands of the Koreans so that Doug and Nell could follow them to some point or place that was important to them. That was the goal. Me surviving the transaction – or not – was irrelevant. Played no part in it.

This was not rationalizing or projecting; it was a subtle reality, one that gave me a sense of peace. Or purpose. There was a point to my death. It would put things right, and make things better for others. A noble death. I began thinking about my life, the moments, and their quality. I was proud of it. A full life of forty-one and a half years. Sure, some bumps along the way, but no regrets. Fulfilling. Rewarding. Satisfying. Justified...

"Don't go there," said Nell. She was looking straight into my eyes again, inches from my face, with a focused determination that put me off.

"Where?" I asked, but I knew she knew where my thoughts were.

Nell put both her arms around my waist and maintained the intensity of her look. "There's something about you, Trippy. Can't put my finger on it, but I think I might want to."

"Want to what?"

"Put my finger on you."

"After we shoot him," said Doug, who was now sorting through the duffel bags on the bed. "Other than that I have no say in the matter."

"Which means we need to keep you alive," said Nell with that penetrating stare.

I realized I was being seduced, but I've always been a sucker for seduction. I was getting the impression that Nell was a chameleon, capable of becoming anything, or anyone, whatever it took to see her goals through to completion. At the moment, I was whatever it took. I objected to her tactics, hated being the reason for her latest change of color, and loved all of the attention.

"You know," I said, "I've wondered who you are, almost from the beginning. But now I'm wondering if you really know who you are. I mean, when you look in the mirror, who stares back at you? I don't think you know."

To her credit, Nell didn't flinch. My words hadn't stung, or given her pause for thought. At least she hadn't shown it. Rock solid intensity. And then I realized she had probably been here before, in this very situation. Was practiced at it. Part of the camouflage. Part of what it takes to be a good chameleon. Which she was.

Her lips suggested a smile. "You'd be surprised what I know about myself, Trippy."

"Yeah, but do you like any of it?" I said.

That brought the smile out. "I like the parts you like."

I wanted to smile back, and I was, on the inside. But the gravity of the situation prevented my brain from firing any smile neurons, so I just stood there, enjoying the moment of looking deeply into another person's eyes. Because it had been a long time since anyone had given me the opportunity to do that.

"Put your sweatshirt back on, lover boy," said Doug. "And keep the vest on. Don't take it off until you've been shot." He was at the edge of one of the queen beds, bent over one of the duffels, both hands inside it. "Now comes the painful part."

Nell dropped the seduction act and threw my sweatshirt into my face. I slipped it over my head and found Doug standing in front of me. He was holding a small plastic bag, clear, and about the size of a Post-it note. He held the bag up and jiggled it. There was something even smaller inside. "This goes in your ear."

It was a one-way transmitter disguised as a mole, brown in color, with what looked like human hairs sticking out of it. To make it look real, Doug told me. When activated, I could hear them, but couldn't say anything back. I wondered if that would become one of those minor details that became incredibly important later.

The painful part was how the transmitter was fitted into the ear, and after Doug used the tip of his Buck knife to turn the thing on, he showed me the small needle at the base of the transmitter that would be jabbed into the inside of my ear.

"It has barbs on it," he said, referring to the needle part. "Hurts a little going in and a lot coming out. Stays in your ear that way."

*   *   *

My ear was still aching from the piercing Doug had given me to secure the transmitter, but the worst part was that he had applied super glue to the back of my ear, which the needle had penetrated, in order to stop the bleeding. Which, it turns out, was what he had meant when he said it would be painful coming out. Not because of the barbs on the needle, but the glue's adhesive properties.

The two of them had then corralled me into the suite's bathroom to test the device. It worked well enough, but hearing Nell's not so subtle sexual references inside my head via radio transmission was beginning to annoy me. I was just another job to her, and her overtures were striking me as cheap. Insincere, at the very least, and just like that, I no longer found the woman attractive.

Which was colossally unfair.

Because she was.

My brain, on the other hand, was actually feeling hopeful. On the short trip in the Mercedes from the hotel back to the Carillon, I learned that the boat from which they were planning to take the shot that would probably end my life was, in fact, a container ship. A relatively stable platform, when it came to shooting people, Doug said. Technically, it was a feeder ship, which meant it was small as container ships go, at six hundred feet in length, and about fifty feet across, but one that had been anchored just outside Los Angeles Harbor for the past three days because of some issue with US customs, an issue the two of them had arranged to persist for at least another twenty-four hours. Perfect for our purposes, Doug had said. From that vantage point, and the increase in elevation, the shot was, in his words, 'a walk in the park'.

My heart refused to harbor any of my brain's hope. While having that eye-to-eye with Nell in the hotel room, I had made up my mind that this was how my life was going to end. It served as the absolute lowest of expectations. The bottom line. No other outcome could be worse; things could only get better, and that was more comforting than knowing an increase in elevation improved someone's chances of shooting me without killing me. This wasn't about me, I reminded myself; it was about Trent and Darcy Hayden.

Your Life Matters.

It was close to one in the morning. We were sitting in the marina's parking lot in front of the gate that led to the Carillion's slip. Doug had turned the car's engine off, and both he and Nell were turned in their seats to face me. I had just asked how they knew the Koreans would come looking for me tomorrow.

"Wouldn't you?" said Doug. "They already tried once; they're bound to come looking for you again. Besides, we got twenty-four hours to play with."

"It's like fishing, Trippy," Nell said. "We're gonna cast a line out and see what we catch."

"And I'm the bait," I said.

Doug said, "You have a real knack for this kind of work."

"No I don't."

"Just go sailing tomorrow, Trippy; Leave the rest to us." said Nell.

Jesus Christ.

Where was the feeder ship going to be, I had asked, and how will I know it's the right one? What if there's more than one container ship at anchor out there tomorrow morning? Doug tapped his ear and smiled. I had forgotten not only about the mole transmitter I was wearing, but the ache it had caused in my ear as well. It's amazing how effective the brain is at blocking out pain. Especially when it senses the potential for an even greater amount of pain yet to come.

"Do you at least know the name of the ship you'll be on? I asked.

"As a matter of fact, I do," said Doug. But then he had to think about it, like he didn't really know. "It's called the *D Star*, short for Death Star." Doug immediately looked to Nell for validation. She gasped, mouth open with joyous surprise. She held up a hand. Doug high-fived it.

That was not the real name of the ship and I was done with these comedians. I opened the door and was out of the Mercedes when Doug added, "Don't forget: five hundred yards or less. And stay in the cockpit."

I said nothing. I slammed the door and walked to the gate, opened it with my key and stepped through, letting the gate slam noisily behind me. I didn't look back. *D Star. D for death.* Screw these idiots.

My heart sank as I approached the Carillion. The orange-yellow light coming from a pair of night lights on the dock revealed the cabin hatch was slid back and the companionway doors were wide open. I was fairly sure I hadn't left it like that. Positive I hadn't. I began looking for damage as soon as I stepped onboard, starting with the cockpit area, but saw no indication of it. In fact, everything looked as I had left it. The winch covers were still in place, and the winch handle and the control lines I had left neatly coiled in a canvas bag hanging against the side of the cockpit were all undisturbed.

That left the cabin, which, from my current perspective, was nothing more than a gaping black hole that held at least the possibility of someone being down below, waiting for me. That gaping black hole was also where my Duracell 1300 was, a foot-long flashlight that would have also served as a pretty effective weapon. And the matches. And the Bic lighter I used to ignite the oven range burners. Anything and everything that would shed even the tiniest light on the cabin's contents was down inside the gaping black hole.

Except for the little keychain light my sister had given me for Christmas a while back; a disc about the size of a poker chip in the shape of Han Solo's spaceship. I had never used it, except as a keychain, and since that was at least two Christmases ago, there was a good chance the battery was dead.

It worked perfectly as soon as I figured out how to activate the tiny thing and a diffused halo of light pierced the cabin's darkness. I thought about leaving a thumbs up review on the manufacturer's website and eased myself down the companionway steps until my hand reached the wall-mounted electrical bank on the starboard side of the cabin, just above the nav station. I was fully expecting to get clobbered on the head from behind, but instead found the switch I wanted and flipped it.

DC-powered light filled the cabin.

I was alone.

But the place was a wreck. Not damaged or destroyed, but tossed. Like the guards used to do to our prison cells when they were searching for contraband. Anything that was once stowed away in a drawer or a cabinet or on a shelf was now on the floor: dishes, silverware, nautical charts, cups, towels, books, cans of food, spare parts for the engine, clothing, toiletries. Every seat and berth cushion that could be removed had been, and was on the floor.

It would take me hours to figure out if anything was missing, but the first place I looked was the storage under the nav station table, because that was where I kept the engine key. The space was empty except for a couple of pencils. So I started searching the floor on my hands and knees and five minutes later found the key and its squishy floating keychain under a plastic dish plate which was under one of the long cushions for the saloon's bench seat. Which meant at least the boat was operational.

I put the long cushion back in its place and sat down amidst the mess. Of course I knew what they had been after: the plates, which were still in my back pocket. Which meant most likely nothing else was missing.

Which meant whoever had been here would be back.

I was too tired to care. Too fed up, too beat down, too burned out. Too angry. Too powerless.

I stepped over the clutter to the cabin hatch and slid it shut, then pulled the companionway doors closed. On my way back to the only seat with a cushion on it, I flipped the interior lights off and used the Han Solo keychain light to avoid stepping on anything I might break. I fell into the seat, stretched out along its length, and wondered if this was what Trent had meant when he had talked about the subtle differences between your life being upside down and it being inside out.

Despite the chaos all around me, and the counterfeit plates in my back pocket, and an ear ache, and a bullet-proof vest that felt like I was wearing a linoleum floor, I was asleep within minutes.

Chapter Nineteen

It felt like the middle of the night and my toes were cold. Because I had fallen asleep right there on the saloon bench seat. Without a cover on me. I don't care how hot it might be during the day, it always gets cold on a boat at night. Has to do with its proximity to water. Which was why my toes were cold. I didn't remember taking my shoes off, but there my toes were, the white-socked tips of which I could just barely see without lifting my head off the cushion.

And the gang members. Two of them, or at least their silhouettes, courtesy the filtered orange-yellow from the dock lights. At exactly the same time that I propped myself up on my elbows, a flashlight snapped on to my left. My flashlight, the foot-long Duracell 1300. Which revealed a total of six gang members all crowded into the Carillion's cabin with me.

One of them was perched on the seat opposite my head. He was wearing a beanie, and it was pulled down to just above his eyes. It was the guy seated next to him that was holding the flashlight – my flashlight – pointing it down to the floor of the cabin. The other four were standing. All of their heads were shaved clean, and I assumed there was no hair underneath the beanie either.

"Good morning, Mr. Deason," said the guy with the beanie. He smiled at me. "First and foremost, I wish to extend my sincerest greetings to you this morning. And to apologize for interrupting your slumber, and for the chaos we may have caused to your boat. But we have a pressing matter to discuss with you, and time is of the essence."

No one had called me Mr. Deason in about twenty years, so the guy with the beanie had my attention, besides his unexpected presence in my cabin in the middle of the night. And his friends.

"May I offer you some coffee?" he continued.

"Who are you?" I asked.

He smiled again. "I think you know who we are. And we know who you are." The guy wearing the beanie then held up a hand and waved with his fingers. A gang member who was standing produced a thermos while another one held out a Styrofoam cup. Not from my boat; I don't believe in Styrofoam. Coffee was poured and the cup was handed to me. Politely. Respectfully. With practiced precision. Like I was their guest and this group was accustomed to entertaining guests.

I thanked the person who handed the cup to me and took a sip. It was hot and tasted fresh. Better than Starbucks. Almost as good the Italian roast via my French press. It didn't matter if it was drugged or poisoned: it was six against one, and besides, I need my coffee when I first wake up. Even if it's poisoned coffee in the middle of the night.

"We are not holding you responsible for the death of Joker," said the guy wearing the beanie, "but somehow his business got mixed up with your business, and we're here to straighten all of that out."

"Joker...you mean Pete," I said. "My client from Friday?"

The guy wearing the beanie smiled. "We couldn't help but notice that the two of you had the same associates. The man and the woman in the Mercedes."

Associates. I took another sip of the coffee, and I think I nodded while doing so.

"Joker was in possession of some items of value at the time of his unfortunate and untimely death, and since he is no longer living, we respectfully request that those items be returned to us. Otherwise we respectfully request that we be compensated for the loss of those items."

"That sounds entirely fair to me," I said, and then took another sip of coffee. "But I hope you understand that I'm not really in a position to make a decision like that."

"You know what?" said the one wearing the beanie, and his hidden eyebrows arched up as he smiled again. "We had arrived at that very same conclusion. But we were hoping you might be able to relay a message to your associates." The smile disappeared. "We're counting on it."

It was the first hint of menace since the conversation had begun. Well, okay, having six gang members visit you on your boat in the middle of the night is in itself adequately menacing. But I mean as far as gestures, or expressions. Or words. I don't scare very easily, but, having done prison time with these types of people – gang members – I understood the swift efficiency with which they operated. And therefore appreciated the scare factor. They were exact and precise, and always fully accountable. Admirably so. Nothing was done unless it was sanctioned, but everything that was sanctioned got done. Without emotion. More like a business practice. This conversation was a business negotiation, and considering what was at stake – a limitless supply of counterfeit hundreds that, in Nell's words, could pass through a bank without a problem – it was big business.

"I can do that," I said.

The guy wearing the beanie was smiling again. "Would you like some more coffee, Mr. Deason?"

I smiled and held my cup out. It was that good. As the guy with the thermos poured a refill, the guy with the beanie brought his hand up again and waved his fingers. The guy sitting next to him handed him a cellphone, which was then handed to me.

"This concludes our business for the time being, Mr. Deason." The guy wearing the beanie then stood up, as did the guy next to him. "Would you like us to help you clean up your boat?"

"That won't be necessary," I said.

"It would be our pleasure," he said.

"It's very nice of you to offer, but I think I can handle it."

The guy with the beanie smiled. "Make sure you give us a call. The number is programmed into that phone."

"Thank you," I said.

"No, thank *you*," said the one holding the flashlight.

Then he said something in Spanish, I think, and one by one, they all exited up the companionway stairs, into the cockpit, and off the Carillion. The last one to exit was the one with my flashlight, which he turned off, and delicately placed on the nav station table. The unexpected visit was ending as it had started: silhouetted gang members, courtesy the orange-yellow of the dockside night lights.

I took another sip of coffee, and marveled at the fact that all of this seemed to be making sense.

Chapter Twenty

Have you ever had one of those days where so many things go wrong that you're no longer surprised when something else goes wrong? Yeah, me too. Maybe it had to do with the time of day, or not getting enough sleep and subsequently not having enough caffeine in my blood, but the whole encounter with Pete's – aka Joker's – people had been surreal; serving me coffee; offering to help clean up the mess they had made. It was difficult for my brain to see it as something else going wrong. The guy with the beanie and his crew had been polite, respectful, even professional. It wasn't something else going wrong as much as it was a complication to what had already gone wrong. Using my last name with a 'mister' in front, for example. Which was scary in itself. The fact that they knew my last name, but they had had unfettered access to my boat for god knows how long, so I guess that was to be expected.

After finishing their second cup of coffee, which wasn't poisoned or drugged apparently, I had checked my watch to learn it was just past five in the morning. Not the middle of the night; more like the moment before dawn. And I had a big day ahead of me – the day I was scheduled to be shot. Like having a molar extracted. I'd have to remember to record all of this in the ship's log. But that could wait. Until after I was dead. I had some cleaning up to do.

I started in the v-berth and worked my way back. It impressed me that nothing was broken or damaged. Like that had been one of the instructions the guy with the beanie had given to his crew before they started tearing the place apart. *Don't break anything. This is someone else's boat and I want you to treat it with respect while searching. Treat it like it was our boat.* I found myself thinking that if I had to have my boat tossed, I would want it done this way. Because it made the cleanup easier.

I had no idea how Doug and Nell had arranged for the plates to come into Pete's possession, nor was I aware of exactly how or why Pete was going to hand them over to the Koreans. Or how and why he had ended up dead instead. That whole connection eluded me, and probably would forever. But it seemed to me if they were going to shoot him, it would be after they had the plates in their possession, not before.

Maybe some sort of double cross.

I had wet a towel and was on my hands and knees mopping the floor of the now restored cabin when a rather probable scenario unfolded in my brain. Something the guy with the beanie had said. Pete's business got mixed up with my business. Either give us the merchandise back, or compensate us for it. *This concludes our business. Request that we be compensated.* Pete wasn't going to just hand over the plates for free. He had expected to be paid. A business transaction. The Koreans get the plates, Pete's people get paid. Everybody wins.

The North Koreans had attempted a double cross. Pete got shot, but not before stashing the plates somewhere out of their reach. Which was where I came into the picture.

And that was when I realized that, all things considered, I probably would have ended up being shot no matter how this whole thing played out. If you followed the logic lines through to completion – somebody shot Pete dead, most likely the Koreans; the Koreans intercepted us on the water with machine pistols, most likely intent on shooting anyone in their way – it became apparent that guns and bullets were the primary tools being used to conduct business in this particular slice of the world. Maybe not logic lines. More like assumption lines, if there is such a thing.

Whatever kind of lines they were, a pre-planned shot while wearing a bullet-proof vest suddenly started making sense. It was a perverse version of getting ahead of the curve. Maybe Doug and Nell really did know what they were doing. Like they had done this before. The Chicago thing, for instance. I know, it was stupid, but there my brain was, starting to place just a speck of trust in the wisdom of Doug and Nell.

"Good morning, sunshine!"

It was Doug's voice in my ear, and it startled me so much that I jumped up from my knees and smashed my head into the underside of the nav station table. Which tipped over the Duracell 1300 flashlight the gang member had placed there – lens end down – which then rolled off the table and landed directly on the bones in my spine before reaching the floor.

It was also creepy; I had just been thinking about these two, and suddenly his voice was in my ear. I had forgotten about the ear-mole transmitter.

Naturally.

"What do you want?!" I said, angry, resentful, before remembering they couldn't hear me.

"Do us a favor, Trippy," he continued, "Stick your head out so we know you're onboard."

I stood on the third step of the companionway so my head was just above deck level, looked towards the marina parking lot, and held a hand up. With the middle finger prominently extended. I then shook my hand. For emphasis.

"Nope," said Doug in my ear. "Wrong direction. Guess again."

I didn't. I returned down below and rubbed the top of my head. I was hoping there would be a lump, because that would justify how much it hurt, but there wasn't. I rubbed it anyway.

"We'll be in position in less than an hour, Trippy."

I looked at my watch. It was almost seven.

"Remember," said the voice, "no more than five hundred yards."

Like I would forget that most important point, the minimum distance for me to get shot without dying.

I was beginning to feel anxious. Something like butterflies meets nausea. About everything, but mostly about what it would feel like to take a bullet in the chest. Was the chest the best place to get shot? Maybe a stomach shot wouldn't be so bad. More padding, less bone. But there were organs to contend with. A shoulder shot would be great, but that seemed like a more difficult shot to make. That would be luck, because the shooter would be aiming for the largest target area. Chest to stomach area. Right in the solar plexus. Which could stop my heart. And kill me. Just my luck to get shot while wearing a bullet-proof vest, which prevented the bullet from penetrating, and still die. From a heart attack.

The shooter: a guy that could make the shot blindfolded. That's what Doug had said. My brain refused to think about anything else. You know how they say to get your mind off of it? There was nothing else in my brain to switch over to. And nothing in my stomach except gang member coffee. The gang that wanted compensation. Or the plates. Which I still had in my back pocket.

When was the last time I had eaten? So I focused on accomplishing at least that. I rummaged through the cold storage and found a crate of eggs and a stick of real butter, both of which threatened to make me vomit on sight. The thought of any cooked food did. I needed something that would counteract the acid created by the anxiety that was being catalyzed by the gang member coffee. Something dry.

Like bread.

Or a stale granola bar.

I had come across the last of them while cleaning up the cabin, and knew just where I had put them. I pulled two out of a shopping bag from a cabinet in the galley, unwrapped them both, and started force feeding myself.

Too dry. Needed something to drink. Like milk. Coat my churning stomach and neutralize the acid.

There was no milk. Trent had finished it yesterday morning.

Trent and Darcy Hayden.

Being held hostage until Doug and Nell saw the plates turned over to the North Koreans.

Which was predicated on me being shot, which started the whole butterflies in nausea loop all over again.

I pulled a bottled water out of the galley's cold storage and guzzled it. Then I sat down at the nav station, and began squeezing the empty water bottle in my hands because I liked the crunchy popping sound it made. Because it went well with feeling sorry for myself, which was what I was doing at the moment. With good reason.

Not rationalizing or projecting.

Just feeling.

I am a positive person. As a general rule, I don't dwell on the negative. Even when I was in prison – a negative environment if there ever was one – I made it a point to rise above all the bullshit, all the negativity, and make the best out of a pretty dire situation. It had made the difference. My attitude changed, and magically, so had everything else. This current situation was no different, I told myself. A better different.

That shift in attitude, that moment of it, in prison.

Weetco.

I had been feeling sorry for myself back then, too, stuck there in a prison cell, and was complaining about it. Loudly. Annoyingly. Which is not something you want to do in prison, because no matter how bad you think you've got it, there's always somebody in there, usually right next to you, who's got it worse. In my case, it was a guy about my age who was doing a life sentence. I couldn't recall his given name. He went by Weetco, which was an Indian word for crazy, because he was part Indian. The Native American kind. A white Indian. Reddish blond hair down to his butt. He wasn't crazy. Just as normal as you or me, until the day he got into an argument with somebody and stomped the guy's head in. We all have days like that. Except for the stomping part. So they convicted him of attempted murder. Life sentence. But with the possibility of parole.

Which was what Weetco had chosen to focus on. The possibility. Not the negative. I had asked him what his secret was, how he managed to stay so positive, despite the ugly prospect and depressing surroundings. 'Learn to focus on the things you can control', he had told me, 'and you increase your chances of surviving the things you can't.' Which, coming from a guy with a life sentence pretty much impressed the hell out of me. My whole prison sentence was less than four years. When Weetco passed that advice on to me, he had already been down for nine. No end in sight.

I had taken it to heart at the time, and the ancient prison wisdom had made the difference. Now I was wondering when I had forgotten it. And why. Because now more than ever it was applicable. I wondered if Weetco had ever made it out to freedom.

Because I felt the need to thank him in person.

Chapter Twenty One

I pulled the San Pedro chart down from a shelf and unrolled it across the nav table. Yes, I have that same chart on my laptop, but analog was faster, in this instance. I didn't need to plot a course. I knew where I was, knew where I would be going, and had a good idea where Doug's container ship – the *D Star*, D for Death – would be located. The harbor has designated anchorage areas for situations like this, where container ships could drop anchor and hang out for a while; I wanted to see it on the chart. Just as I found the defined polygon, a voice called out to me.

"Trippy. You up?"

It was a real voice, not from the mole transmitter, but from out on the dock. It sounded like Redman, a prospect that represented a bunch of unfinished conversations and unanswered questions. And therefore suspicions. It was seven on the dot. A bit early for visiting, so this would be business of some sort, the Redman version of said. Which meant I was busted. He had probably seen Doug and Nell at the boat. Or me standing in the parking lot in the middle of the night. Getting dropped off by a Mercedes. Or maybe it was the gang members he'd noticed. At four-thirty this morning. All six of them. And caught the whole thing on video.

So busted.

I laid the Duracell 1300 onto the chart to prevent it from rolling up on itself, which it did anyway, then went to face the music, which, in this case, was a funeral procession.

I hopped up into the cockpit. Redman was standing on the finger slip, smoking a cigarette.

"You're smoking," I said. Judgmental.

Redman exhaled a cloud of smoke. "You're the one who bought 'em for me."

I rescinded my judgment and smiled. "Are you enjoying it?"

"Three a day," he said. "The addiction's in your mind, Trippy."

"Pretty sure there's a physical component to that," I said.

"We'll see." He took another drag on the cigarette which was pinched between his thumb and index finger. It looked unnatural. He exhaled smoke. "How was your client yesterday?"

This was weird. Redman being polite and conversational. He was being social. "Awesome," I said. "The guy took to sailing like fish to water. Made my job easy."

Redman just stood there, smoking the cigarette with focused incessancy, inhaling it, holding the smoke in longer than you should, then exhaling. Which was the type of behavior you'd expect from Redman, but at the same time, could indicate there was something else brewing inside that head of his. Could go either way from this point.

After a moment of him doing absolutely nothing but smoking, I finally asked, "Was that it?"

"Pretty much," he said, and took another hit. "Except that I also wanted to apologize." Exhaled.

Not typical Redman behavior. Too social. "For what?"

"For the way I acted in front of Hayden the other day." Hit. Exhale.

I was shocked. And considering the path my life had taken recently, the concept of shock had an exceedingly relative value. I had never heard Redman apologize before –

left. I couldn't remember the last time I had charged it, but that hardly mattered now. I didn't have Doug's number anyway. Didn't want Nell's.

Seventeen hundred yards was just under a mile. That made five hundred yards over a quarter of a mile. I looked for some landmarks that might help me reference the distance. There were none, except the seawall which was too indistinguishable to be of any use. There was the channel entrance behind me, and a red channel buoy on my starboard, but they were both too far away. I'd have to rely on the GPS waypoint and my position relative to the feeder ship. I used the phone's calculator and my brain to figure out that at my current rate of six knots an hour, I'd cover about half a mile every five minutes.

Doug kept counting the distance down in fairly regular intervals, and when he called out five hundred yards, I dropped a waypoint into the handheld GPS, and slipped the engine into neutral.

"That's your outer limit, Trippy. You still got the vest on? You better have the vest on. And remember to stay in the cockpit."

I went below just to piss them off. I was sure they had binoculars on me, and the thought had crossed my mind to moon them or something, but I supposed the situation was too serious for that. They would find it funny, of course, but I wouldn't.

"You're a real comedian," said Doug. "Anyway, you got nothing to worry about yet. No sign of the bad guys."

Hearing that made me realize that perched on the deck of the container ship, Doug had a three-sixty view of the surrounding area, which meant they'd be able to give me a heads up if any other craft were approaching. Including the Coast Guard. Relatively speaking, that was only mildly reassuring.

* * *

An idle mind is the devil's playground, and after an hour of waiting for something to happen, my mind was exceedingly idle. At first I played with the boat and the GPS, taking her out of the five hundred yard range, then timing how long it would take me to cover the distance until I was back in range. Then I motored up close to the feeder ship, flipped a U, headed away from her, and then slipped the engine back into neutral. There was no wind, but I unfurled the jib anyway and watched it flap aimlessly for about ten minutes.

There had been absolutely no other traffic worth mentioning, and Doug had been silent the whole time. I appreciated that. I thought for sure he'd be feeding me stupid jokes. You know, because I was a captive audience. Or that Nell would get on the radio and start talking about how she wanted to bang me, and that would have really pissed me off. Because I did find her attractive, but only in a physical sense, and I'm the type of guy that has to be attracted to the brain as well as the body. Honestly, it's all about personality when it comes to women. You take a hot chick that beats her dog and instantly the heat dissipates. But that might just be me and the way I feel about dogs.

It was bothering me that I was attracted to her. And that she was pretending to be attracted to me. For the sake of the job. But most of that burden was on me. I hadn't been interested until she expressed interest. Okay, that's not true. But when I first met her, she was with Doug. I don't hit on women in relationships. At least I don't any longer. My second wife was married when we first started flirting. But when I realized that Doug and Nell's relationship was purely a working one…of course by then she had already ruined it all. Offering herself as a prize if I'd take a bullet for them.

I pushed Nell the chameleon out of my mind and began wondering what was going through the minds of the Koreans. Did they know I was out here? Why didn't they hit the boat when it was slipped? Had they given up or lost interest? Was it possible to lose interest in an infinite amount of legitimate, passable, hundred dollar bills? Maybe there was a more practical reason. Or a logistical one.

My phone rang. I dug it out of my pocket and looked at the number. It was an unusual area code. I answered it.

"Oh captain, my captain!" said the voice.

"Who is this?" I asked.

"It's your favorite first mate! And I'm ready to go sailing again!"

It was Trent. "My god, Trent! Are you alright?"

"Of course! Why wouldn't I be? You mean with things here in the office? Sure. That all blew over and I'm back in the coal mines. Did you get the letter I sent?"

"You're in the office?"

"Yep."

"In Philadelphia? How did you get away? Did they release you? What about Darcy? Is she alright?"

"What in the world are you talking about, Trippy? Of course she's alright." Did you get the letter?" he repeated.

"But I thought you were... I thought there was an accident and--"

"How do you know about that? Wow, word travels fast these days. Yeah, yeah, we're both fine. It was just a fender bender. We missed our flight, but we caught the next one out. Took the red eye. Went straight from the airport to the office."

I had no response. Because I thought Trent and Darcy were having their fingernails removed. They weren't. They were back home.

"You okay, Trippy?"

All I could manage to say was, "My battery's low."

"Don't trip, Trippy. Call Perry. He'll tell you all about it. You are gonna love it! Our way of saying thanks. Call me back when you're charged up again!"

Trent disconnected.

It was a trick. The whole thing was a trick and I had fallen for it. Doug and Nell had pressed me into service on a false pretense. An effective one at that. The real problem was that I didn't know what to believe anymore. The Koreans, the plates, the whole arrangement of getting me shot because that would sell the transaction. There was no end to the possibility of deceit.

Right then, I knew exactly what I had to do. I jammed the transmission into gear, pushed the throttle forward until the engine was revving at three thousand rpms, and pointed the Carillion back to the marina.

Chapter Twenty Three

If you've ever been punched unconscious, then you know that most likely you remember the punch, and remember waking up on the floor, and nothing in between. I woke up thinking about the Carillion and all those bullet holes punched in her side. I was thinking how serious that would be, and how it was essential that the holes be plugged up before the boat started taking on water. My brain was having problems determining whether that was imagination or reality, like it knew that thought could exist in my mind without it being true. My brain was having lots of problems of that sort. Like maybe it had been doped up. Because everything was rushing into my mind out of sequence, and I couldn't get a handle on the timeline. Which made sense, considering all the damage to my body. My left arm was in a cast, from just above the elbow to the middle of my hand, and my right leg was wrapped in bandages in two separate places, the thigh and the calf. The left arm made sense: I had banged it against some part of the boat. But was that before or after I got here?

I couldn't still be onboard the Carillion. Because last I remembered, there were chunks of her flying around down below. Wood and fiberglass bouncing around with pieces of lead creating dust and damage that I knew would be fatal to the boat. This boat was different. Clean and dry, and upright, which was when I recalled the Carillion had begun to list heavily to port. Boats only list when they're taking on water.

Doug and Nell in my ear, and Koreans with guns onboard, after the plates, which I remembered being airborne just about the same time I was. And smashing my arm into the side of the companionway after a baseball bat to my chest lifted me off my feet. Except it wasn't a baseball bat. The vest, which I was no longer wearing, and the cast on my arm, which wasn't there before. Okay, so that was then, and this is now, and I had no idea how much time had elapsed between those two memories.

My head was hurting so much I was getting sick to my stomach.

She must have gone down, in the outer breakwater anchorage.

But I am here, and this is not the Carillion.

Maybe my eyes aren't really open.

Maybe I'm not awake.

My brain was turning itself off.

Trippy

A night of dreamless sleep and I was feeling fantastic. I was awake with my eyes closed and was wondering if this was what meditation was like. Everything was just One Thing and there was a pinpoint singularity about it. I was apart from that One Thing. It was there, hovering, and I was me, stationary, grounded.

I was pulling the thought of the Carillion out of and away from that One Thing so that I could look at it. It was its own thing, and I could pull separate thoughts apart from the Carillion thing. I saw components, and thoughts about those components, as two different things. Like they were bundled that way – by me. And if I chose to do so, I could rebundle them back together in different ways. The thoughts had emotions connected to them, and I was putting the emotions aside so I could see things as they really are, without having to feel the emotion. The boat's engine was a component of the boat and I pulled that apart and discovered thoughts about the engine that were mine. They were not the component, not the engine, but thoughts that I had attached to the engine. And emotions attached to the thoughts. Because I had decided so.

What clarity! Such facility! There was the engine, and the oil running through the engine, and a thought about the condition of the oil in the engine, which came with an emotion about its condition, or rather came with the thought of its condition, and I was holding all of these in my head, separated from each other, but with an understanding that they were relative to each other. Not bound unless I chose to bind them, a decision-action that was effortless and natural.

This can't be making sense to someone who hasn't experienced it, but it was as though I was looking at another person's life, their joys and problems, examining those associated thoughts, and was therefore unattached to the emotions that were bound to them. I understood that there could be emotions – should be – but I was free to consider those thoughts without the burden, or relief of the corresponding emotion.

So when it occurred to me that all of this was in the past, when I realized that the Carillion was no longer, and therefore had no engine, or at least no longer the need to consider the condition of oil within the veins of that engine, it was without remorse or regret or guilt or pain. I was free from all of that.

I was liberated from it, and the concept of liberation reinforced that One Thing, that wholly connected singularity, of which I was a part, and yet not. And I suddenly had a most curious thought: one meditates to arrive at this sense of wholly connected, singular liberation.

And that was reassuring, except now I wasn't so sure I was awake.

Chapter Twenty Four

Nothing was making sense.

I had stirred to consciousness at least twice to find myself in the v-berth of some boat I didn't recognize, only to be overcome by either nausea or fatigue or pain, and consequently slip back into the relative comfort of sleep. The third time I awoke, I had no choice. I was too thirsty.

I started with the shelf that lined the sides of the v-berth I found myself in, and discovered a plastic grocery bag on the shelf to my left. In it was a bottle of pills whose label said they were three hundred milligram Vicodin; a smartphone; my watch, and a bunch of paperwork that I didn't bother reading because all I wanted was something to drink. I left the bag in the v-berth and started figuring out how I could get from where I was to anything that had liquid in it. Like a faucet in the galley, or maybe the head. With my good hand, I shoved aside the blanket covering me and discovered I was completely naked. So I turned back to the shelf of the v-berth in hopes of finding clothing. There wasn't any.

I didn't mind that there was a cast on my left arm. Or that my right leg was practically useless. Either injury by itself would be manageable. But the fact that these were opposing injuries made getting in and out of the v-berth of a sailboat – naked – a technical challenge. Not to mention walking. I discovered that the right leg could support a degree of weight, but any flex in the calf muscle created a searing pain that told me it wasn't happy about being used. Too bad; I needed something to drink.

    Thank god for the hand holds and grab rails built into the interior of this boat. I used every single one to make it to the boat's galley, where I found a cold storage compartment that held a chilled six-pack of bottled water. I grabbed the whole pack, drained two of them in a row, and immediately got sick to my stomach. From the headache, I figured. So I took a break on one of the seats in the main saloon until my right calf started throbbing. I was admiring the craftsmanship of the boat's interior and fighting the urge to throw up at the same time, when I noticed a pile of folded clothing on the bench seat just to my right. One was a black t-shirt with a picture of the Death Star on the front, and a pair of Wrangler jeans, both of which still had the Wal-Mart price tags stapled into them. No underwear.

    My body was a wreck, but my brain, thank god, was finally starting to put thoughts together in the proper sequence, despite the incessant pounding between the temples. I had gone from being knocked unconscious aboard a boat that was most likely sinking, to sitting here, in this boat, which didn't even feel like it was on the water. Which was when I realized I didn't know where I was. I mean geographically, where the boat was. I stood up on my only good leg and looked out a window in the main cabin. I immediately recognized the boat next to me, a Pearson thirty-two. I was in my slip, the Carillion's slip, except this wasn't the Carillion. I one-legged it to the other side of the boat and did the same visual check, and saw the Grand Banks cabin cruiser that had been there since I took this slip five years ago. I was home. I was also getting sick again. I returned to the seat next to the clothes.

    This boat looked new, and it felt that way. The wood paneling was much lighter in color than you'd find on older boats, and the interior fiberglass materials looked clean and blemish-free. All the seat cushions were fresh and crisp; not matted down or misshaped or worn, and the light fixtures were all recessed into the coachroof of the cabin, and equipped with what looked like halogen bulbs. It was a very nice boat. I wondered if this was Doug's, or maybe Nell's. Or maybe the people they work for. Government people. A government boat. Maybe this was where they stashed people after they got shot delivering counterfeit plates to foreign governments.

My headache was killing me. I reached up to massage my temples and discovered what felt like bandages wrapped completely around my head. I needed to see that. The ship's head was directly across and to the left of where I was sitting. I hopped over on one leg and stepped in. I didn't recognize the reflection in the mirror. My entire head was wrapped in white gauze, there were dark circles under my eyes, and it looked like I hadn't shaved in over a week. Smack dab in the center of my chest was a bruise the size of a basketball. It was purple and black with splotches of ugly yellow. The bullet impact. I probed the top of my head to determine where the actual damage was, and found it at the back, almost dead center. At least that's where it was the most sensitive. I wanted to unwrap the whole mess and take a closer look, but my stomach had other plans.

I managed to get the toilet seat up just as I vomited mostly water. I swore softly between another two retches. The throbbing in my right calf wouldn't quit either, so I waited to make sure I was done throwing my guts up, then headed back to the v-berth, grabbing the clothing and the remaining bottles of water on the way. By the time I was back up and onto the lumpy cushions of the v-berth, I was physically exhausted. No wonder I'd been sleeping so much. I took one of the throw pillows, wedged it into the shelf on my right, then turned my body so I could prop my damaged leg onto the shelf. The throbbing eased almost immediately, and I prayed my head would do the same. At least my stomach had decided to settle down. Got its way when it threw up.

I couldn't get the timeline straight in my head. I thought I should remember getting a cast wrapped around my arm. And my head bandaged. How long does that take, and where do you do that? In a hospital, right? Or an urgent care? The head and leg injuries might have been field dressed, but the cast? Obviously a medical professional had tended to my injuries, but why couldn't I remember that?

The head wound.

Amnesia?

I reconstructed the pertinent events as best I could in a brain that was reluctant to participate: on the boat, surrounded by guns and Koreans, getting shot, presumably by Doug and Nell. Or their people. Blacking out. Now here, all bandaged up. Amnesia was a possibility, but it might also be shock. I knew a guy who had survived a pretty nasty car accident. Drove his van off a cliff. He didn't remember any of it, just woke up in the hospital, asking what happened. The doctors had told him it was the shock blocking his memory. Some sort of self-preservation instinct. But I didn't even remember the hospital part. So I was sticking with the amnesia theory for the moment.

I gave the timeline in my head a day. And a night. Twenty-four hours to get off a shot-up and sinking boat, rushed to a hospital, examinations, x-rays, the cast, all the medical stuff, then brought here. All courtesy Doug and Nell, I was assuming, the only two people who probably knew exactly what had happened, but were nowhere to be found. So, a full day for all of that to happen, which would make this Wednesday, the twenty-second, because I was positive it was Monday when I got shot. I was comfortable with that. Temporary amnesia. I made a note in my head to google that condition, to see if there were such a thing. Which was when I remembered that this wasn't my boat; my computer wouldn't be on it. Nothing of mine was on this boat.

Both my heart and my brain were in agreement about the Carillon: she was gone. It was a prospect, like when someone

Chapter Twenty Five

The intent was to confirm the date, you know, make sure I hadn't made a mistake. My watch didn't have one of those date window things, but all smartphones keep an exacting record of time. And dates. Automatically. Not something you set yourself. Comes from the network. Accurate to within a second or something.

So there was no doubt in my brain when the display reported the date as being Sunday, the twenty-sixth.

The bastards had stolen four days from me. Four days, because I was willing to give them the one day, which would have been last Tuesday. Which left Wednesday through Saturday, giving them enough time to get their story straight. Which was when I realized I wasn't suffering from amnesia, or maybe I was, but it had been induced. Chemically. Which would account for my other physical symptoms: crazy headache, nausea, and a penchant for sleeping twelve hours like it was an afternoon nap. And those bizarre dreams. Doug and Nell had sedated me for a few days while they set everything up, sorted everything out.

And suddenly everything was making sense, with a level of clarity that was refreshing. *This is what we do for a living, Stupid, and we're good at it.* Yes they were. I went back through the paperwork piled on my chest and checked all the dates again. The constructed timeline was a seamless, leak-proof cover that slipped snugly over the facts, and smeared the truth along the way. So you couldn't tell the difference. I wondered how deep it went, whether if I called the Santa Barbara Police they'd have an accident report in their files that matched the one I had in my hands. Or whether the yacht brokerage would have a record of the sale of the Carillion and the purchase of this boat. Or the hospital, and its line-item invoice for medical services rendered.

Of course they would. Child's play for these two. And they'd had nearly a week to put it in place. *What we do for a living.*

Stupid.

There were two other documents within the mess of paperwork that I'd missed the first time around. The first one was the temporary DMV vessel registration paperwork verifying that I was indeed the owner of a new boat, presumably the one I was now on. Also dated the twenty-first. The last one was a joke, of the practical variety, courtesy the same two idiots who had stolen at least four days of my life. It started with the letterhead of the yacht brokerage company at the top, Seacoast Yacht Sales, in Santa Barbara, and below that, a typed letter:

> Dear Trippy:
> It was a pleasure working with you to help you find your dream boat. If you have any questions regarding your new vessel, please feel free to call our offices; we'll be glad to answer any questions you may have.
>
> We apologize the delivery process took longer than expected, but we're sure you understand that your unfortunate auto accident and your week in the hospital was a delay that none of us had anticipated.
>
> Hope you're feeling better!

Kind Regards,
Doug and Nell of
Suncoast Yacht Sales

Underneath that, someone had written in blue ink:

Saw the cast off Jul 1
Pull your stitches tmrw
Leave your head alone
No doctors
Under the cushions!

And below that, a crude drawing of a heart being pierced by an arrow, followed by:

Told you it would work!

And then another heart, this one with the initials D and N inside it, a plus sign between the two.

Yeah, that part was true; they had told me the vest would work. Must have slipped their minds that I'd be losing a few days of my life as well. Or maybe that part wasn't planned. Maybe they only blacked you out when things went south, you know, like when you get your arm broken and you get knocked unconscious, and you're left for dead on a sinking boat. Maybe the blackout was Plan B. And that made sense, too. People like Doug and Nell always had a Plan B. Specialized in it. Like boy scouts, or something.

How do we get Stupid to play along? I know! We'll knock him out for a week! Give him amnesia! Like a week-long blackout!

Which was when I flashed on Penny Page, or rather the young Penny Colski, who was all too familiar with what blackouts were, and how she would never recall that particular evening when we met because she had overdosed on alcohol and god knows what else. I thought about the kinds of drugs government agents would have access to.

Truth serums and knockout drops and all sorts of chemical cocktails that could render you unconscious for hours. Or days, four of them in a row. A pinprick, or a bottle dropper, or a dissolving tablet slipped under my tongue while I was still unconscious onboard the Carillion. Or pills that were labeled as Vicodin, for the pain, but were in fact Amnesia pills. It was more than just plausible; it made sense, of the perverse variety. It was the kind of thing that people like Doug and Nell did. Like faking a kidnapping in order to dupe a Good Samaritan into doing what seemed like the right thing.

Which always came with consequences.

I was enraged and impressed. Grateful and pissed. The nice young couple who had lied about miscarrying a baby had put my life in mortal danger, and then saved that life. All in a day. And, they threw in a boat, like a consolation.

Because I was keeping the boat, and I had the paperwork to prove it.

I grabbed the empty plastic shopping bag, and while cramming all the papers back inside it, began wondering if I was their first victim, or if this was the way they always operated: sweeping into people's lives, turning things upside down and shaking until every little thing came tumbling back out and smashed to the floor, and then put it all back together again, not in the same order, but close, and with perks.

Who does that?

Who were these people?

I picked up the phone and studied the photo of Doug and Nell. He was sneering, and she had bunched her lips up, like you do when you're blowing someone a kiss. What a senseless waste of a great set of lips. How many times had she used those to get what she wanted?

I wanted to throw the phone but figured I might need it, since my phone was probably on the bottom of the Pacific Ocean. So I grabbed the bottle of Vicodin pills which I now suspected were amnesia pills, if there was such a thing, and threw them with my right hand as hard and as far as I could aft. The bottle hit the inside wall of the cabin I was in, and bounced back onto the cushions right next to me. Because I'm left-handed, the hand that was in a cast.

And that pretty much summed it all up: throwing the pills had been the right thing to do.

As usual, it had come with consequences.

* * *

I had no idea how long I had been asleep when I was rudely awakened by music. It was Darth Vader's theme song, you know, that somber, one note at a time passage they played whenever Vader was about to do something evil. I couldn't figure out where it was coming from until I felt something vibrating against my left thigh. It was the phone. I fumbled to pick it up and saw a number on the display that looked vaguely familiar. I answered it.

"You on the water?"

It was Perry Jennison, and I was flat on my back still staring out the hatch at a now twilight sky.

"Perry." I pulled the phone away from my ear and looked at it. Not my phone. "How did you get this number?"

"You gave it to me. About seven years ago. I redeemed your share of Sandfall Paradigm."

"My what?"

"The stock certificate. From Trent's company."

Which triggered the memory. The call I was on when all hell had broken loose onboard the Carillion. Just before that. Perry had called to tell me Trent had given me a share of something.

"What about it?" I asked.

"Like I said, I redeemed it. Last Friday."

"For how much?"

"A hundred shares of Alphabet."

"Alphabet?"

"Google. Which is Alphabet now. Google bought Sandfall Paradigm," said Perry.

I reflected on the significance of this. Trent's company had been bought by Google, and I wondered if that was what Trent had wanted. I couldn't remember if he had expressed an interest, one way or the other, only that the issue was the essence of his problems. The finance guy with problems. How long ago that felt. And then I remembered Doug and Nell had lied to me about kidnapping Trent and his wife. And that Trent had also called me while I was aboard the Carillion. Which was when I had learned he wasn't really kidnapped. Which was why I was out of range. All of which felt like yesterday, but was a week ago.

"What's the date today?" I asked Perry.

"The twenty-sixth," he said. "Why?"

Of course the date on the phone was correct. Four days missing. "When did you get the letter from Trent?" I asked.

"Same day I called you. Last Monday, I think."

"And that was the last time you and I spoke."

"You don't answer your phone," said Perry. "I assumed you were on the water. Out of range. Is there a problem?"

Perry was getting impatient with me, annoyed with the conversation. Because I wasn't making sense.

"I was in an accident," I told him.

"Accident? What kind of accident?"

Which was when I realized that the cover story Doug and Nell had built for me was infinitely easier and more sensible than the truth. More plausible. Because otherwise I'd be explaining to Perry and everyone else in the world that I had been shot while wearing a bullet-proof vest while delivering counterfeit plates to the enemy. Which made no sense at all. And couldn't be proven. And yet, stuffed in a plastic grocery bag was all sorts of proof in the form of written documents that indicated I was involved in a car crash in Santa Barbara that resulted in injuries. A week ago. Substantiated it. Legalized it. Authorized it.

start counting the blessings bestowed by those two? Besides the boat, which I was definitely keeping. Counting Doug and Nell as a blessing was a stretch. But there was mom's voice in my head, telling me to count them anyway, even if they were of the stretchy variety. Because you never know.

The concept of gratitude has the unique ability to divide the world up into two types of people: those who always manage to somehow move beyond the tragedies that beset them, and those who never seem to. The grateful and the ingrates. Both types make that tragedy a part of their life, one the foundation for greater things, the other a great weight that presses down on them, making everything else smaller, less significant. Thanks to a set of parents that insisted on gratitude, I'm the first type. Which doesn't mean I'm destined for greater things; I just don't like being pressured by stuff, don't like things weighing me down. From practice. Because you get pretty good at moving on, at turning tragedy into opportunity when tragedy is all you're given to work with. That's why people who fail a lot – but keep trying – tend to succeed, if that makes any sense. They get good at recovering.

I was well-practiced in recovering, and with two sets of stitches now pulled from my right leg, my body was recovering.

*   *   *

It was becoming my mantra: *they had thought of everything*. Like a well-stocked galley that ranged from your everyday items such as hot dogs, buns and relish, to exotic stuff I wouldn't even know where to buy, like cans of Petrossian caviar, packets of smoked salmon from some outfit called Duck Trap, and wheat crackers from Switzerland that had expired about a year ago but still tasted amazingly good.

Who loads a boat up with Euro-food? Or EMT-grade first-aid kits? Or fourteen thousand dollars in cash?

Which was what the handwritten note at the bottom of the phony brokerage letter had meant when it said *Under the cushions*. As in *look under the cushions, Stupid*, which I did, eventually, but only by accident, because it felt lumpy. There was a manila envelope – again – but in this one, along with all the non-counterfeit cash, was a white, sealed envelope addressed to Pete, and a four-foot electronic cable of some sort. Pete's envelope felt thin, too thin for money, but just about right for a single sheet of paper.

The cable made sense because also underneath the cushions was a laptop computer, the real source of the lump that had first started me exploring. And that's where the real surprise was hidden. Inside it, between the keyboard and the screen, was a handwritten note, on stationery from the Pike Hyatt hotel. The handwriting was different, more feminine than the printed lines on the brokerage letter:

> You are one of the bravest people I have ever met, and I've met a lot of brave people. Most only think they are, but you are the real deal, Trippy. And for all the right reasons: loyalty, friendship, love. If I could, I would like to get to know who you really are…you know…when you look in the mirror. Maybe some other time?

It was signed simply with an N.

I suffer regularly from Lonely Puppy Syndrome. Anyone who pays even the slightest attention to me becomes the sole object of my affection. Over the years, I've fallen madly in love with dozens of complete strangers, just because they were nice to me: supermarket cashiers, bank tellers, a lawyer, a prison guard, even a tow truck driver named Angela, who was nice enough to show up in the middle of the night to give my Rabbit a jump. I'm a sucker for kindness, and here Nell was, being kind to me. The woman I thought I hated, wanted to hate. Hated hating.

Who was this chameleon, who clearly didn't have a heart but was all of a sudden showing one? What kind of person does that? Who thinks of everything, including leaving a cute little note that suggested there might be more to this than just a casual encounter? What goes on in a brain like that? How does that brain reconcile itself with its beating heart? I wanted to know.

In fact, I wanted to know everything I could about Nell. And Doug, for that matter. And whoever they worked for. I wanted to know how they did it, how they managed to think of everything and not miss a thing, and why, and for how long they had been doing it, and who was next on their list.

I wanted to know if I would see her again.

Of course, that was the lonely puppy in me.

Because I did know the type. Nell and her partner Doug were gone. They had cleaned up and dusted off, leaving absolutely no trace behind. Which is what people who think of everything for a living do.

I thought about that for a moment. I thought about calling the boat brokerage, or the Pike Hyatt, or maybe tracking down every single brand new Mercedes S500 AMG registered in the state. Or maybe finding out who had requested that the feeder ship be delayed by customs for just one more day. There had to be something, some clue, some trail I could follow that would lead me to…something.

Or someone.

I could hire a private detective agency that would look into the falsified police report and hospital medical bills. I would tell them the whole story, whether they believed me or not, and let them do a little digging. They didn't have to believe me; I would be paying them to do it, paying them to believe me. After all, I could afford it. Trent and Darcy, for instance, were bound to have some sort of record from the auto accident, like the name of the guy that hit them and made them miss their flight. His insurance company, or maybe a driver's license number. Trent could do some computer thing and hack a database and do a records search. Or a facial recognition thing. Because I had their photos. It was possible.

Anything was possible.

I was rich.

If I could I would like to get to know you.

Maybe some other time.

I read the note from Nell another four times, and was about to read it again when I realized the whole love affair I was having in my head with Nell was becoming one of those crushing weight things that consumes your every waking thought to the point of blotting out reality. Squishing everything else into oblivious insignificance.

Focus on the things you can control.

There's a difference between putting it behind you and letting it go. You can put a tragedy behind you and then, eventually, let it go, but not the other way around. Because once you let it go, well, it's gone. Unless you've experienced that sort of tragedy, it's hard to even understand what it means to do either, put behind, or let go. I had put my four years in prison behind me, but refused to let it go; it was too precious to me, meant too much.

And so it was with the girl named Nell, and her partner Doug, who had shot me and stolen nearly a week of my life. And sank my boat. It was time to put it all behind me, but still there. Those things in your life you put in front of you tend to block your path, your progress. I couldn't have that. I needed to move on, dragging whatever I couldn't let go of behind me.

And it was precisely at that moment that I had decided to move on, with all of the events of the past seven days, all that baggage, trailing behind, griping, grumbling, angry and heartbroken, that I heard someone outside, out on the docks, calling my name.

It was Redman.

Chapter Twenty Seven

Redman wasn't buying any of it, but for all the wrong reasons. I had been arguing my version of the story long enough that the sun had gone down, and he was still convinced that my new best friend and multi-millionaire Trent Hayden had something to do with the new boat. Because Redman had been following the story online, the 'Google Buys Sandfall Paradigm' story, which I guess was really big news in Redman's world, and therefore hard not to follow. And while it was virtually impossible for him to counter the fact that I had a cast on my arm and fresh wounds on my head and leg, he wasn't for a second buying the accident in Santa Barbara thing. Despite all the evidence in the plastic grocery bag, which I had shown him.

Intimidated is such a strong word, and I think it would be unfair to say that Redman was intimidating me. Accurate, but unfair. Not in the menacing sense, but the way he would cross his arms and get really quiet and dead-stare me for minutes at a time.

"It's the way you're telling the story that makes me suspicious. Like you rehearsed it," he finally said after an epic dead-stare moment.

I held up the plastic grocery bag. "What about this?"

"Photo editing software, a decent printer, and an Internet connection, I could have you scoring the winning try in the 1987 Scottish Rugby finals."

"The what?"

"The touchdown. It's called a try in Rugby. You gonna tell me, or do I have to find out for myself?"

"You'd never figure it out," I said. "Because it is too unbelievable to be believable."

"Why don't you start with the Chinese."

"Koreans," I corrected him, which prompted another crossed arm, muted dead-stare. "You're guessing," I added after about ninety seconds of stony silence.

"Speedboats, machine pistols, wraparound glasses, the guy with the bloody head. And a close call with the Coast Guard," Redman announced.

It was probably the look on my face, because just like that Redman was now validated. Smugly so. "There is no way you faked all that just to impress a client," he said. "The logistics alone would make it practically unfeasible. And the cost, unless you happen to have some Korean friends who own an offshore racing boat and had nothing better to do on a Sunday afternoon."

"Trent," I said.

"I friended him on Facebook. Surprisingly, he accepted."

"You're on Facebook?"

Answered by another haunting dead-stare.

So I told Clive Redmond, the sailing derelict that everyone knew as Redman, whom I'd never seen actually go sailing, the whole story from start to finish, and even pulled up my shirt so he could see the splotchy purple, black and yellow bruise on my chest. Not for him. I didn't do it for his sake, but for my own. Because my conscience was telling me it was the right thing to do. Because of the consequences of never telling anyone.

"So where's the Carillion?" he asked.

"Sunk. On the bottom. I don't know."

"You don't know where your boat went?"

"I was unconscious."

"Was it sinking when you were not unconscious?"

"On its way," I said.

"Do you know how hard it is to sink a fiberglass boat? It's like trying to sink a Clorox bottle with the cap still on it. Fill it full of holes, and you might submerge it, but send it to the bottom? No way."

"You don't understand, Red. These people are good at what they do. They're pros."

"Pros? Pros at what?"

"At everything," I said. "Good at everything, think of everything. Like shooting a guy in the chest standing on a boat from another boat five hundred yards away. Maybe more."

Redman went silent again, but the stare was redirected, no longer on me, like maybe he was adding things up in that dangerous brain of his.

"Okay," he finally said. "I'm gonna go get a cigarette, and smoke it on the dock, because I don't want to smell up your new boat. And maybe when I get back, you'll tell me what really happened."

Redman got up from the saloon seats, and was heading for the companionway steps.

"How am I going to do that when that's what I just told you?" Redman was at the top of the companionway, about to step into the cockpit, and I said, "Red, wait."

Which, amazingly, he did. And then he started backing down the companionway, backwards, and slowly, feeling his way down the steps without looking where his feet were going. Which I thought was awkward at the least, if not unsafe, until I saw why he was doing it that way.

It was the double barrel of a sawed-off shotgun, and the gang member holding it, at the top of the companionway steps.

The gun was pointed directly at Redman's gut. The gang member followed Redman down the companionway, and behind him came another gang member, also armed. And then a third gang member appeared, weaponized. The procession kept up until there were once again six gang members and at least six illegal firearms in the cabin of my brand new boat. The one I had decided I was keeping, because I had earned it.

I recognized the sixth guy. He wasn't wearing his beanie, but his head was indeed shaved. The other five made a path to allow the guy without the beanie to move forward until he was standing directly in front of me. Redman was back to sitting where he had been, except now the sawed-off shotgun was pointed at his head. The guy without the beanie noticed the cast on my arm.

"Good evening, Mr. Deason," he started. "I believe we have some unfinished business."

"I had an accident," I said.

The guy without the beanie smiled, but just for a second. "I can see that. I hope that you're comfortable. Are you in any pain?"

"No, no. I just meant that was why I hadn't got back to you. The phone you gave me; I lost it."

"Most likely when your boat sank, I would guess."

"You saw it sink?" I asked, astonished.

"From a distance." The guy without the beanie smiled again.

I looked to Redman, because now I was feeling validated, and I wanted him to know it, but his undivided attention was fully focused on the burred tip of the shotgun barrel poised six inches from his nose.

I looked back to the guy without the beanie. "I think my...associates left me something to give to you."

The guy without the beanie's eyebrows arched up. "Really?"

With planned deliberation, I reached over to the plastic grocery back on the seat next to me, and fished through it until I found the sealed white envelope with Pete's name on it. I handed it to him, and he handed it to the gang member standing next to him, who I think was the same guy who'd considering I only had one good arm and one and a half good legs, I left the engine running, and hopped onto the dock so I could truly appreciate the mellifluous sound of a fifty-horse Volvo Penta diesel, with less than a hundred hours on it, burbling at idle.

Which was when I noticed the name painted on both sides of the boat, as well as on the fold-down transom of the stern.

D Star.

In thick, stylish, black letters, with my home port San Pedro (pronounced by the locals as *Peedro*, by the way), underneath.

D for Death, as in Death Star.

It was the cherry on top or icing on the cake or whatever other cliché you can think of to describe the last and final stroke of what seemed in my opinion to be a masterpiece. An inside joke that only three people in the world would ever get, would ever laugh about, could ever appreciate.

And for just a brief moment, I was back to those questions that had nagged me from the beginning: who were these people? Who thinks of things like this, those *everything* things? Who lies about a miscarried baby, about kidnapping your friend and his wife, and then takes the time to change the name of the boat so it matches some private part of your life that will stay with you forever. And leave what I was now convinced was an unrequited love letter. Who else could take what most would consider a series of tragic events and, in the end, make fun of it, like wasn't that a blast, and gee, I hope we get to do that again someday.

Who sends *maybe some other time* notes after they've shot you in the chest?

I had relegated my brain – and my heart – to never knowing the answers to those questions, and that's a lot easier to say than it is to do, like so many other things in life. Because I still had all these little reminders, like a cast on my left arm, or having to pay over a hundred dollars to the dealership for a new key to the Rabbit, getting a replacement driver's license, replacement ATM card, changing all the passwords for my online banking, four hundred dollars for clothing, including underwear, and about a thousand other little tiny things that reminded me that my entire life had been turned upside down and shaken with measurable force until everything that was, wasn't.

Of course, I had the boat, and the fourteen grand in cash, which was now down to eleven, because I also needed a few more things for the D Star – D for Deason, I told anyone who would ask – and in my possibly damaged brain it was pretty close to a fair exchange. Besides, where would I begin? The local police? My congressman? Imagine how far that complaint would get once they found out that the guy making said complaint was an ex-felon. An ex-felon who was now the owner of a boat he hadn't paid for, and couldn't afford anyway, according to his tax records of the past five years. Which would inevitably lead to the discovery of the eleven grand in cash in a manila envelope hidden away on the illegal boat. If the cops didn't start asking the wrong questions, the IRS sure as hell would.

Which brought me back to Mom, advising me to be grateful for what I did have, and to not stir the pot, or bite the hand that had fed me, or some other homespun honeybee Reader's Digest wisdom quote. So I shut up about it, pretty much, and watched with just a pinch of regret as everything faded into the fabric of my past in a relatively short period of time. All the tragedy and resultant triumph, the perks and penalties, the promise and the pitfalls.

Everything except Nell, but I was guessing that she, too, would gradually slip behind me so that I might be able to let go, albeit gently, reluctantly, longingly.

Maybe some other time, said the lonely puppy inside me.

you're on. If you think about it, divorce is always the beginning of a new life, and the end of an old one. No doubt Shannon was viewing it as the end, while her husband and his penis were probably viewing it as that chance to begin again. The truth, naturally, is that it is both things for both people. It's all about perspective, something Shannon was severely lacking at the moment. I couldn't blame her.

Shannon turned out to be a neat freak, or something along those lines. It started as soon as we were onboard the D Star, because there, in the cockpit, were two steering wheels, side by side. She wondered if it required two people to steer the boat, so I explained to her how sailboats sail – leaned over to one side, leaning opposite the wind's direction of travel – and how it's easier to see where you're going when you're standing on the high side of that equation. She thought that was a remarkably efficient way to build sailboats – duplicity, she labeled it, which does not mean a double of something, by the way – and her enthusiasm persisted as we ventured down below where she discovered that the stove was built on a gimbal, so that when the boat was doing that leaning thing, the stove and its associated pots, kettles and pans would remain level. She literally shrieked with joy and amazement when she found the latches on every cabinet door that prevented them from swinging open unexpectedly and dumping their contents on the floor.

Which is exactly what Shannon did an hour later, except it was her heart and soul that swung open unexpectedly and began dumping. We had just transited the San Pedro breakwater under power, because there wasn't any wind yet, as usual, and were seated in the cockpit, each of us behind our own duplicitous wheel, discussing her line of work, which was not strictly psychology but more like a life coach for troubled but affluent teens and their disconnected parents – her phrasing – when something clicked inside the poor woman's head, and it all came out. Probably if I had been paying attention to her, I would have seen it coming, but she had those clown-sized sunglasses on, which meant not only could I not take her seriously, but I also couldn't see her eyes, so the whole episode caught me by surprise.

She dumped her life on me in one long lament that ended up with rivers of tears flowing down her cheeks, which, when mixed with the makeup and the blush and the rouge and that eyelash stuff, formed what I was sure was some chemical solvent that would forever stain the cockpit's sole. I'm being honest here; that was my first reaction, which meant my second one was I needed a towel to mop that shit up before it ate through the fiberglass and compromised the integrity of the boat. At least on the inside. On the outside, I was nodding sympathetically and making sounds of disgust and disapproval as Shannon told me how Jason her husband had been sleeping with a bunch of people that Shannon knew personally, not all of them women, which seemed to hurt Shannon even more. Men are pigs, I consoled her, with the disclaimer that I had been a pig more than once in my life, and the future wasn't looking very bright for any sort of reformation in that area.

Surprisingly, this helped Shannon, or not so surprisingly, because that's what sympathy is, or does. My confession that I had sinned in my past, but was now in remission from said sinning, apparently gave dear Shannon some sort of false hope that she latched onto with startling ferocity. Equally startling was her sudden epiphany that I was understanding and compassionate and honest and genuine and a good listener, and I knew instantly where this was going, so I suggested that since Shannon was feeling better about things that we raise the sails and see if her refreshed outlook might help us catch some wind.

Fortunately, Shannon had no reference for what amount of wind constitutes good sailing, so the fact that there was just barely enough of it to fill both the main and jib sails made us both happy. The boat's Volvo Penta diesel did most of the work, but Shannon didn't know that. I did, however, something ex-felon's brain as it ventured into the tumultuous waters of mid-life crisis.

I followed the sessions on the workout video faithfully for exactly seven days, at which point my brain started threatening to stop feeding signals to my body if I kept this reckless idiocy up. The jump rope, however, offered a nice compromise. I placed the jogging mat squarely on the D Star's foredeck just forward of the mast, set the fitness watch timer for thirty minutes, and hit the rope.

I nearly died after four minutes.

The Internet told me what I was doing wrong, and after adapting something called an interval workout, I managed to lose five pounds by the end of September. I didn't care about the weight so much, but loved the fact that all my jeans and shorts were beginning to feel loose on me. I also had a bunch more energy, and nothing to expend it on.

Despite September being one of the most desirous months for sailing in Southern California, with a perfect combination of blustering squally winds, white-capped waves and bright blue skies, it is historically one of the slowest months for charters, at least according to the spreadsheet I used to track my monthly sales, one of the few files I had bothered to regularly back up to a free cloud that came with my email account. Which meant no clients, which meant I quite often had nothing better to do than punish myself by working out, eating food that started green in color and then went bad, as opposed to the way the food in the D Star's galley normally aged, and stare at my body's painfully gradual metamorphosis in the tiny rectangular mirrors built in to the sliding doors of the medicine cabinet in the D Star's head.

In other words, I was bored to death.

There was a call from Perry, who suggested I diversify, which I later learned meant not keeping all of my money eggs in the Google basket, so I did that, sold fifty of my Google shares, which I kept forgetting was called Alphabet now, and parked the cash in an online brokerage account until I decided what else to spend my money on.

Coincidentally, on that same day, Shannon Friedly called to tell me the blank check I'd been holding was worth twenty-two hundred. She had settled for twice that amount in monthly alimony, plus the title to the house, the mortgage for which Jason would be paying for the rest of his puny-dick life – her phrasing – and half of his IRA. *By the balls!* she interjected into our conversation repeatedly, with perhaps a bit more enthusiasm than I was comfortable with, although I was genuinely happy for her. I begged her not to pressure me into cashing her check right away, suggesting that twenty-two hundred was a bit much for a pleasant weekend of sailing. *A deal's a deal*, Shannon blustered, and then proclaimed the only thing she would ever pressure me into was sex, after which she laughed loudly, informing me this was her new approach to life in general, and it seemed to be working. *You go, girl*, I said, and we disconnected, but not before reminding each other to never lose faith in love.

*   *   *

Despite my exercise regimen and consequent improved state of health, I had somehow, over the slow period in September, developed the slovenly habit of falling asleep every night in the main saloon with the forty-inch TV on, mostly because I discovered that the CD/DVD player built in to the D Star's entertainment system was Blu-Ray compatible.

So naturally, I picked up a copy of one of Jenny's movies, which turned out to be the one I had already seen, the one where she plays a con artist, because it was under seven bucks at Wal-Mart, and the only other DVD of hers I could find was some trilogy for nearly forty bucks. I wanted to see if she looked the same, you know, on film versus real life, and on this particular night, the last thing I remembered before drifting into sleep was that angelic face, frowning and pouting, and gracing all forty inches of the flatscreen TV Lenny's card had bought me. And yes, I was envisioning her naked, standing right in front of me.

Chapter Thirty Three

I was awakened suddenly and violently, and it took me several seconds to recognize who was standing over me, their hand on my shoulder, rocking me awake. I kept blinking my eyes, trying to make sense of what I was seeing, trying to process the shock.

It was Doug, or what was left of him, and when it finally did make sense to my brain, I screamed out a religious expletive.

His face and head were covered in a mixture of blood and sweat. His nose looked broken, offset by a quarter inch from its straight line to the nostrils, and there was a two-inch, flapping-skin gash on his left cheek oozing blood, the drops of which were falling onto my chest. His left eyelid had been sliced open vertically, also bleeding profusely; his right eye was swollen shut. The entire right side of his face was grotesquely misshaped, as if it had been artificially inflated. Blood was dribbling from his forehead in scattered rivulets, over and around the eyebrows, down the bridge of the broken nose, and forming droplets at the tip which fell onto me with rhythmic consistency. His right ear was mangled badly, a tangle of bloodied pink flesh with white cartilage sticking out where it shouldn't.

"What the fuck happened to you?"

Doug said something, or tried to, his bloodied and distended lips spitting out a spray of blood that peppered my face.

"NOW!" he finally managed to get out. "You have to leave now!" His expression was desperate, more so by the grisly damage. He grabbed my blood-soaked shirt with one hand and pulled me in close to him. "They're going to kill us! Leave now! Leave now!"

His only visible eye wavered, drifting up towards the damaged eyelid. "Christ, Doug, you need a doctor!" I scrambled out of the saloon seats and to my feet, his hand still clenched on my clothing.

"No!" he said urgently. "No doctors! Just leave! Right now! No time!"

Then I noticed his arm, the one he wasn't using. There was a deep spiral laceration more than six inches long that ran from just below the inside of his elbow nearly down to the outside of his wrist. A hole was torn through the back of that hand, between the thumb and index finger. Like a bullet had passed through it.

"Jesus Christ!" I could see the bone beneath the cut in his arm.

"Never mind that," he said, a flash of mania in his slashed eye. He released his hold on me with a shove. "Go! Get out of here as fast as you can."

I headed to the nav station to retrieve the key to the engine. Doug's good hand spun me around.

"Don't come back until I tell you to." Doug faltered for a moment, like maybe he was about to lose consciousness, then regained his focus. "Not until I say so."

"But where? Where should I go?"

He grabbed the top of my shoulder and squeezed hard, like maybe he was using me to maintain balance. "Doesn't matter. Nowhere. Anywhere. Just stay out there, on the water, away from here, away from everywhere. No place is safe. Do you understand me? No place!"

He grimaced in pain, and I moved to support him, to stop him from collapsing right there. He recoiled back, then locked his stare on me, his face drawn and pale.

"I'm sorry, Trippy, I didn't --" He abruptly let go his grip on my shoulder and looked around, alerted, as if he had heard something.

"Now!" he said, then headed towards the companionway stairs, limping painfully up them and out to the cockpit.

"Doug! Wait!" I started to follow him up the companionway stairs.

He turned back to me, his face tormented. "Leave now or you're dead." he said gravely. He jumped from the cockpit to the dock and landed hard, almost falling to the ground, then broke into a staggered run up the dock towards the marina gate.

My whole body was accelerated from the adrenaline pump. I couldn't think clearly. I knew I needed the key to start the engine and was turning back to retrieve it from the nav station table before I realized the key was already in my hand. I hopped up and into the cockpit in time to see the tail lights of a single car speeding out of the marina parking lot. I jammed the key into the boat's ignition, cranked the engine until it caught, then jumped down to the dock and threw off both mooring lines.

Back onboard, I shoved the engine into gear and pulled forward out of the slip and into the channel. I looked back over my shoulder, expecting all hell to break loose, in the form of gunfire, or people running down the dock towards me, or maybe Doug, coming back, his injuries overwhelming him. But none of that happened. I did a three-sixty. It was still and quiet; I could see no other person anywhere. I was the only one operating in panic mode at the moment.

Something was beeping, and it took me a moment to realize it was coming from my fitness watch. My heart had reached and was sustaining the preprogrammed target heartrate: one hundred forty beats per minute.

"Jesus Christ." I played with the buttons on the watch to silence the beeping, then brought up the current time on the display: two-fifty-four am. There was absolutely no doubt in my mind that Doug had perceived imminent danger. Christ, the damage to his face alone was sufficient to convince me the threat was real. The Koreans? Had something gone horribly wrong in their otherwise perfectly planned, efficiently executed operation? How was I the key? Why would they be targeting me? Maybe it was the boat. Maybe it was stolen, and the rightful owners wanted it back. No scenario was making sense.

My heartrate had settled down to something just over a hundred when it dawned on me that I hadn't prepped the boat for departure. The dock fenders were still hanging over the side. I made sure the D Star was centered in the channel, then raced over to the port and then starboard sides of the boat and retrieved the two black rubber cylinders. I left them laying on the deck, and scanned the horizon in all directions for any possible threat. Mercury light from the hundred-foot-tall shipyard light towers on either side of the channel painted the water and land in a surreal orange. I saw nothing. No movement, no action, no potential danger of any kind. I was the only vessel in the channel.

I was trying to recall how much diesel there was in the tanks when I noticed all the blood. It was everywhere, glistening orange-black in the artificial light. On my hands, my shoulders, my clothing, my feet, and on everything I had touched since manning the helm. Doug's blood, smeared on the wheel, smudged on the engine throttle, footprints and shoeprints on the cockpit sole, handprints on either side of the companionway bulkhead. Probably both of ours. I thought about Doug, and his chances of survival. He had lost a lot of blood, much of it deposited on the D Star. There was nothing I could do about that. His instructions had been explicit: *leave now. Don't come back until I tell you to. They're going to kill us.*

What if Doug didn't make it? What if he wasn't alive to tell me when to return? What then?

The Vincent Thomas Bridge, silent, and lit up in luminous symmetry of fluorescent blue, was dead ahead, and for the first time I saw it as ominous.

I'd be a sitting duck passing underneath her.

From up there, even a lousy shot with a Big Five deer rifle could fill the boat with enough holes to stop her cold. And kill me. Couldn't miss a forty-one foot sailboat as it leisurely floated by at under three knots an hour.

A chill started at the top of my head and ran down my neck; maybe the adrenaline and the threat of violence, but maybe because all I had on were a pair of boxers and a blood-soaked t-shirt, and it was three o'clock in the morning. I headed below with the intent of grabbing a pair of jeans and a hoodie sweatshirt. The only light below was coming from the soft blue rectangular glow of a TV with no signal. I decided to leave it that way until I nearly slipped in all the blood on the floor. I turned on a bank of interior lights and was stunned by the amount of blood spilled over the cabin sole. There was no way Doug would make it. He had left a trail of blood everywhere he had been.

Which was when I noticed the smeared path of blood leading into the aft port cabin. I couldn't remember Doug going in there. I certainly hadn't. I flipped the cabin light switch on. There was a large black nylon bag on the berth cushions, about four feet long, maybe two feet wide, and just as deep. The blood trail made it clear: Doug had somehow managed to stow the bag in here, despite his injuries, probably before he had awakened me.

My first thought was weapons of some sort; Doug's weapons. Because of the way the bag looked. A black bag full of machine guns, or AK-47's, or maybe more counterfeit money, lots of it, judging from the way the bag was filled. It didn't matter what it was, except that it was most likely contraband, and the cause of Doug's injuries, and my unplanned panicked departure in the middle of the night. There wasn't time to find out. I had to check the D Star's course. She was probably directly under the bridge by now.

With bare feet now freshly inked with a new coat of Doug's blood, I hopped up the companionway steps and back into the cockpit. I looked up to see the underside of the bridge moving slowly past me, and breathed only half a sigh of relief; the shooter could be waiting on the other side, waiting until I passed under. The boat's course was true. I wanted to return below decks, because it would be safer, but also to find out what was in the bag, but there was a turn coming up in the channel, maybe half a mile ahead.

So I stayed in the cockpit and waited. As the outer edge of the Vincent Thomas Bridge became apparent, I looked back and began scanning its perimeter, looking for something, anything anomalous, a form, the sliver silhouette of a rifle barrel, or a figure, a person crouching, or a stopped car. There was nothing. I was tempted to take the other half of that sigh, but instead waited. I focused on my bloodied hands gripping the wheel and realized my whole body was trembling.

Only when the bridge looked to be a hundred yards astern did I grant myself the luxury of breathing. I returned my attention forward and calculated the distance remaining before the channel turn. Maybe another thirty seconds. I used the time to calm down, and my thoughts returned to Doug. The hole in his hand that looked like a bullet had passed through it was the damning evidence. His damages had not been caused by the ordinary, if there was such a thing, like a car crash, or maybe even a train wreck, even though that's what he looked like. No, it was a battle, of the close combat variety. Hand to hand. With weapons. Over what? And where was Nell? Had they separated? Weren't they a team of sorts? That left two possibilities in my mind: either she had nothing to do with the events that had turned Doug into a bloodied mess, or she had, and hadn't survived. Doug was close to being dead, and considering his size and weight, whoever or whatever had done this to him would have done worse to Nell. Much worse.

I waited until the D Star had passed the bow of the USS Iowa navy warship – a floating museum, permanently moored on the starboard side of the channel – then made the turn and set the boat's autopilot. It would be a two-mile straight shot before the final turn needed to navigate the seawall entrance. I took the chance I wouldn't encounter any traffic and went below deck.

The nylon bag had an oversized zipper running down the centerline, and as soon as I had about a foot of the zipper pulled down, I realized it wasn't guns or money.

It was a body.

Long dark hair matted with blood, motionless, on its side, curled in the fetal position.

It was Nell.

Chapter Thirty Four

She was almost unrecognizable, severely damaged, maybe worse than Doug. Her hair, wet with coagulating blood, was stuck to the side of her face. Her clothing was shredded, and she only had one shoe on. Then I saw why: someone – Doug, probably – had attempted to treat an injury; a torn rag, drenched in blood, was wrapped around her left foot.

I didn't know where to start. With a pulse, right? To see if she was still alive, but I didn't know how to do that. I'd seen movies where somebody pressed a finger to a person's neck to check for a pulse, but I didn't know exactly how that was done. Never actually had to do that on anyone. And in this case, her neck was slick-red with blood. Maybe the wrist. I tried to find my own pulse by the wrist, but couldn't.

I pushed the bag down and away, clear of her body. She stayed curled up in the fetal position. Blood had pooled in the bottom of the bag and was sticky to the touch. The body was cut and bruised and punctured and slashed everywhere. The part of her face I could see, her left side, looked like it had been dragged a distance on asphalt or something: a three-inch-wide diagonal scrape with deep parallel lines that had stopped bleeding but were crusted up with a mixture of dried blood, sweat and dirt. I wanted to move the body, get her out of that bag, but remembered enough about first aid to know doing so could cause further damage. Which was a ridiculous thought. She had probably arrived here slung over Doug's shoulder. In the bag, with Doug injured so badly he was walking like a club-footed hunchback. Another ridiculous thought: further damage might not matter, because I still didn't know if she was even alive.

It would have to wait; the D Star's position in the channel. The seawall would be coming up. I hadn't been keeping track of how much time had elapsed.

There was a second turn in the channel I'd forgotten about, or rather the second half of the same turn. Like a dog leg; the first half, a short straight run of maybe half a mile, then the second half, requiring maybe only ten degrees more to the port. But if I hadn't come on deck at just that moment, the D Star would have plowed itself into a sixty-foot catamaran on an end tie in front of a seafood restaurant on the starboard side of the channel. I made the course correction, but it still wasn't the straight shot to the seawall entrance I wanted. I had to man the helm, which stuck me in the cockpit again, behind the wheel, waiting to reach open water before knowing whether Nell was dead or alive.

Doug wouldn't have dragged the girl here if she were dead. No need to. Even if it was to dispose of the body, there had to be a bunch of better places to do that than my sailboat. Which was when it struck me that's what this was all about. Doug was going to come with me, and together we would have dumped Nell's body over the side of the D Star. Maybe halfway between here and the island. In the middle of the night. Like that hasn't happened a bunch of times in this part of Southern California over the past hundred years or so. Fish food. No wonder there were reports of great whites along this stretch of water.

But something prevented Doug from joining me. Had panicked him at the last moment.

No loose ends or whatever.

The people who thought of everything, one of whom was now dead.

She wasn't dead, I started convincing myself, just unconscious, and here I was, standing topside, doing nothing about it. I still had maybe two more miles to go in the channel before transiting the seawall, and if she weren't dead already, she might be by the time I got back down to her, despite my lack of first aid knowledge. So I cracked the throttle open, brought the boat speed up to just under six knots, and returned below.

Nell's body had rolled onto its back, but I didn't know if that was what dead bodies did once they were no longer confined by nylon bags, or if it was a sign she was alive. Then I saw her face, and the sight turned my stomach and enraged me. She had been beaten, but not like she had lost the fight; more like tied up and defenseless while someone went to town on her: lips fat, torn and bloodied, both eye sockets puffed out to bulging shut, pressure cuts on the eyebrows and cheeks. The swollen nose had stopped leaking blood but the diagonal gash running across the bridge was dribbling fresh blood. Maybe not a balled up fist, but a club or bat or metal pipe brought against that fragile face with excessive force. Like they enjoyed it. The rage took hold, and all I could think about was tearing to shreds the person who had done this; smashing their face with my bare hands, caving in their ribcage with steel-toed boots, breaking their cheek bones and crushing their throat. I couldn't stop the thoughts from forming and filling every moment of my existence. Violence for the sake of it, because it felt good and purified me and made me whole. Because it empowered me, and gave me a sense of purpose. I had to fight to get the fury to release, and it was only the thought of crashing the unpiloted boat into the rocks before I had the chance to do all these things to the people responsible that finally broke the lure of unbridled violence.

My brain needed a break from the turbulence of revenge so I returned to the cockpit to check on the boat's position. That sense of purpose and empowerment came along, and started doing the thinking. In a matter of seconds, I was hyper-focused on just two things: consider her alive until you know for sure, and don't do anything until you're out of the harbor: if you crash the boat into the seawall, you'll be useless.

The next thought was getting her the medical attention she needed. It was a question of honoring Doug's wishes to keep Nell off the grid – because that's what it was really about – and maybe risk losing her onboard. If I didn't have what the girl needed medically, her death would be on me. Something told me Doug had already calculated that risk. What they did for a living. Bringing Nell ashore would be more dangerous; it would decrease her chances of living. That's what Doug had meant.

Leave now and don't come back until I say so.

He wasn't thinking of me. Or himself.

The first aid kit was stowed in the port cabin, so I split my time between getting that unzipped and ready, and keeping an eye on the D Star's course. By standing on the third step of the companionway, I was above the deck line and could take sightings on the harbor lighthouse on the starboard side of the breakwater entrance. It looked an hour away, but the math was telling me I had about twenty minutes before I'd be out to open water.

It's strange, but that sense of purpose, fueled by the prospect of gratuitous violence, had settled me. Or maybe it was the fact that I could finally see the dim outline of the gap in the seawall, or that my adrenal glands had finally shut off, but something like a checklist began forming in my brain: secure the safety of the boat; stop the bleeding; survey the damage, begin damage control. I jumped back to the cabin, grabbed the book out of the first aid kit and returned to the cockpit. There was a whole section on treating unconscious patients, and with a flashlight trapped between my chin and chest, I began reading. It started by telling me what unconsciousness was, and listed some of the reasons for it. There were about five causes listed, but the prime candidates in my mind were either *blow to the head* or *severe blood loss*. Probably both. This section of the book assumed I had already checked for signs of breathing, and I felt stupid for not thinking of that. I made it my top priority and kept reading.

By the time the D Star was finally out of the harbor and into open water, I had a procedure locked in, courtesy the first aid instruction book: check the airway, check her breathing, manage her circulation, control the bleeding. And now I had the time to execute it. After making a hard right just beyond the breakwater entrance, I set the autopilot's compass at two-forty, magnetic, which I knew would point the boat just west of Catalina, and went below.

Nell was trying to prop herself up on her right elbow. She must have seen me, or sensed my presence, because she immediately started groaning.

"No, no, no," she said in a voice that was surprisingly strong. It wasn't whining or crying, more like a warning, like this had better stop or there'd be hell to pay.

"Nell, it's Trippy," I said, but it didn't seem to register. She kept saying no, and tried scooting back, away from me, from the sound of my voice, using just the one elbow and a leg to drag herself towards the back of the berth. I kept telling her it was me as I approached, telling her she was safe now, and finally it must have stuck, because she stopped all movement and looked at me like she was trying to see if I really was who I said I was. I doubted she could see much with her eyes puffed shut like that.

Then she collapsed.

I crawled up onto the berth next to her so I was kneeling next to her head. The fury returned, replenished. It was hard to look at her; the last time I saw a face in this condition was prison, belonging to a guy the other inmates were convinced had molested his own daughter.

"You're going to be okay," I said.

She let out a short breath and whispered, "What are you doing here?"

She had asked the question I was thinking, but her tone was one of exasperation, like my presence was only going to complicate matters.

"Don't talk, don't move, just stay quiet," I said. "I need to check you out." Her left hand searched until it found my knee and she pressed her fingers into it. I put her hand in mine and gently squeezed. Which was when I noticed the marks on her wrist; she had been bound, tightly apparently, and by something that was strong and thin, smaller than a pencil, but strong enough to cut through her skin. The wrist wound looked older than the ones on her face, like she had been tied up for a while before they decided to start beating her brains in.

I began a systematic inspection of her body. The arm of the hand I was holding looked uninjured except for the ligature marks. It was severely bruised above the elbow, but the skin was intact, and none of the bones appeared to be broken. Her neck and chest were soaked in blood, but there were no obvious cuts or gashes that I could see. I'd have to wash her down to know for sure. The left arm had a bleeding slash in it, between the elbow and the shoulder, like maybe from a knife, and the pointy part of that elbow was about twice its normal size; I'd have to assume it broken for now. This hand's wrist had a matching ring of dried blood and gouged flesh.

Her torso had escaped significant injury except for the hole in her left side. It looked dangerously deep; a half-inch triangular-shaped puncture wound that was still oozing blood through the thin ribbed cotton t-shirt she was wearing. Wrong shape for a bullet, I thought, but having never seen a bullet wound up close, I wasn't sure. I promoted this to most serious injury, above the possibly broken elbow. The rest of her stomach and chest, or rather the shirt, was wet with sticky blood, but apparently uninjured. Again, I'd have to wash away the blood to know for sure.

I was checking for damage around both her knees because that's where the blood was on her jeans when her hand found my knee again. I looked to her.

"Doug?"

"He's the one who brought you here." I hesitated, unsure she was ready for what I was about to say. "He didn't look good, Nell. About the same as you."

"He went back?" she asked, her brow creasing as best it could.

"I don't know, but he's not here."

"Here?"

"We're on the boat. The D Star, heading out to sea."

Her face relaxed, and something resembling a smile began to appear but quickly faded. She said something, but I wasn't sure I heard it right. It sounded like *I have good taste*, which made no sense.

So I just agreed.

"Yes, you do."

Chapter Thirty Five

Despite her diminished physical and mental state, the girl actually had the balls to tease me about having to strip all of her clothes off.

"Do I embarrass you?" she had asked in a weak and unintentionally sexy voice as I fumbled with the button and zipper of her jeans.

I told her she'd better shut up, and threatened to take pictures if she didn't. I think that made her smile again.

The bad news was her left foot, the one missing the shoe, and it was vying for top priority on the damage list. It looked like she had caught it in a piece of machinery, maybe an industrial garbage disposal or a corn harvester, or something that had shredded it, and there was little I could do about it except keep the leg elevated and control the bleeding with compression bandages. Two hours ago, I hadn't known what a compression bandage was, much less how to apply one, but in that time, I had successfully used butterflies, gauze bandages and compression wraps all over Nell's body. The first aid book, which had become my bible, contained explicit instructions and detailed illustrations for every procedure I attempted, and Nell's improving demeanor was all the validation I needed.

Getting her cleaned up was the unpleasant part. The fifty-fifty blend of saltwater and fresh water was excruciating at times, I'm sure, but it was the closest I could get to what the book called for, a saline solution, and I ended up washing the entire body with diluted seawater just to get rid of all the caked-on blood so I could see what else was damaged. By the time we were finished, all that remained was cleaned, naked skin, albeit most of it punctured, abraded, gouged, sliced or bruised, and now adequately bandaged. The puncture wound on her left side wasn't as deep as I had first thought, so I ruled out a bullet being stuck in there, and even shined the flashlight in it to make sure. I could have used some ice to help reduce the swelling around her eyes and that elbow, but hadn't bothered to fill the little ice cube trays with water – being that I wasn't expecting company – but wet rags tossed on the freezer shelf of the cold storage unit for about an hour worked almost as well.

The berth cushions were ruined with blood. I didn't care about that, but didn't want her lying in it, so with a little effort and a few choice words from the patient, I positioned her onto of a bed of towels, then loosely covered her bandaged naked body with a sheet and kept a blanket nearby. She had the presence of mind – and the audacity – to call me a chicken.

By daybreak, I was satisfied the patient was stabilized – a term I had picked up from the first aid book. She was breathing, had stopped bleeding, and her heart was beating. We were about halfway between San Pedro and the island when she asked for water, which I thought was really good news from a medical standpoint. I used that opportunity to give her a couple pills from a blister pack in the first aid kit that was marked: *Percodan/Aspirin. For Pain as Needed.* The label had a bunch of other warnings on it: contains opioid, not to exceed so many pills in a certain amount of time, take with food. All of which I ignored, because I was a recovering addict with plenty of opioid experience and knew what I was doing.

With a little help, she managed to drink the last two bottled waters left onboard in rapid succession which was real progress until two minutes later when she needed to pee, a condition for which I had failed to plan. I convinced her to use a cup while laid out flat on the berth, because the alternative was figuring out how to get her from the bed to the head without causing more damage or inflicting more pain, and I just wasn't up for that. Neither was she. Thank god for the towels.

"What are you gonna do when I have to shit?" she asked with that crooked, swollen-lipped, half smile that I learned was the modified version of a wide grin. Her courage astonished me. She had to be in pain, and yet, still had that resilience of humor which, combined with the defiant, lopsided attempt to smile, caused me to forget everything else in the world but her.

And the people who had done this to her.

"Girls who look like you shouldn't use language like that," I said.

"Why, do I look like shit?"

I pretended to check my fitness watch. "Wow, you have just used up all of your talk time for the day. I'm ordering you to go to sleep."

"Pillow?" she asked.

Talk about melting. The way she said it with a tiny helpless voice made me feel so important that I realized I was enjoying this role as caregiver just a little too much. I'd rather have her healthy and gone from my life than this, the wounded chameleon. But I gave her a pillow, actually tucked it under her head for her, because I was loving the caregiver thing, then pulled a bucket and more towels out of the portside cabin and headed for the cockpit.

The first light of day is often described in poetic terms as being magical, great for so many things, like the soul, one's outlook on life, or the rejuvenating promise of hope; but blood smeared and traipsed everywhere is definitely not one of them. You would have thought a whole platoon of marines had died in the D Star's cockpit, and the blood, now three hours old, had begun to set, so throwing buckets of seawater on it did absolutely nothing. I went below and returned with a scrub brush, got down on my hands and knees and began scrubbing Doug's blood off the sole of the D Star; puddles of it, splatters, flings, footprints, shoeprints, palm prints. So much of his blood was washing down the scuppers and out to sea I began checking astern for sharks.

In between water buckets hauled up over the side of the boat, which, by the way, get impractically heavy after about the fifth bucket, I realized the real problem was our supplies. It takes hours of careful planning to prepare and provision for a three-day sailing trip; I had no idea how long we'd be gone. Until it was safe to return, Doug had said in a compromised state of consciousness, which could be a long time, or maybe never if Doug was no longer alive. The onboard water tanks might last a week if we rationed, but I wasn't sure rationing was the best thing for my patient. Sure, I owned a desalinator; currently it was sitting in my sister's garage in a town south of us by about 40 miles. As the crow flies. Food – lack of it – would become a problem in about the same time. Taking inventory of current provisions became the next item on my to-do list.

The cockpit finally looked like the blood was gone, but I could still see it, and feel it, so I added the task of bleaching the whole area to the bottom of the ever-growing list in my head, then headed below to check on the patient. She was asleep, a damp washcloth over her eyes, but I put my face close to her mouth anyway to make sure I could feel air going in and out. The injury priorities got reshuffled when I took another look at the left elbow. If it was broken, and didn't get properly set, she might permanently lose range of movement in that arm. The first aid bible had prescribed icing to control the swelling, and I'd done that with the frozen wash rags, but it didn't look like it was helping.

I needed real ice.

The order came from my brain, but I wasn't sure whether it was the good side or the bad side, or god forbid, the two of them working together, which would be a first, but the message was nonetheless clear.

Do what you need to do to ensure Nell's survival.

Doug had duly impressed me that there was danger onshore, certainly for him, and primarily for Nell, it turned out, and I guess by proxy that included me. But did that danger extend to the island? Was it a global danger, or localized? Because if I could slip onto the island, and into the general store at Two Harbors…

No place is safe.

Nell probably had at least some of those answers locked inside her head, but grilling her for the circumstances behind her most recent and clearly punishing encounter seemed not only ill-advised, but bad form as well. I decided to keep her out of the equation entirely.

The back side of the island might work. I could even use the hillsides and the Eucalyptus trees as cover, if needed. Four trips between the boat and the store would be ideal; two wouldn't be enough, because of the water jugs and the bags of ice. So I settled on three trips and started the list. That was the easy part. The hard part was figuring out what to do with Nell; specifically, how to secure her on the boat while I was away. Then I remembered something from my own not-too-distant past, and there was the answer.

I hated myself for even considering it.

*　　*　　*

It ended up being five trips, because everything went as planned, meaning I wasn't kidnapped or shot at or arrested while on dry land, and accordingly, had no need to hide behind the trees and bushes on the multiple trips between store and shore.

Despite the unusual circumstances, I treated this island visit like every other journey to Catalina Harbor: picked up a mooring can, paid the fee to the harbormaster, then took the inflatable to shore and parked it amongst all the other inflatables at the relatively uncrowded dock. Some lady was on the docks waiting for her husband who was on the other side of the isthmus trying to rent scuba gear, so I explained to her what I was doing – making a bunch of trips to the general store – and she agreed to watch over my stuff until her husband returned. By trip number four, the husband was back, loading his own inflatable with tanks and wet suits, which is what allowed me to make the extra run.

The very first thing I did upon entering the general store was pick up a copy of that morning's LA Times. The dominant headline was not the merciless beating of a couple of government agents, but a story about the theft of something called a bitcoin, and how that was roiling the financial markets. I knew nothing about coins, and just a little about financial markets, having only recently learned that Google wasn't really Google anymore. The good news was that neither Doug's nor Nell's photo was splashed across the front page, or any other page, because I went through the whole paper. No accidents, no tragedies, no unexplained deaths or murder investigations, or persons of interest – nothing that I could connect to the two of them getting beaten up. Which kind of made sense, in my mind at least; well established at thinking of everything – and getting away with it. But the lack of immediate notoriety was a relief, nonetheless. It made me wonder what the emergency was really about, the one that had sent Doug fleeing to my boat with his unconscious partner stuffed in a bag slung over his shoulder, the one that had caused him to issue the warning not to return to land until he said the coast was clear.

It was none of my business, I had said to myself, but while motoring the inflatable back to the boat, loaded with jugs of water and bags of food and ice, I realized that it was my business, considering the fact that Nell, beaten to within an inch of her life, and now recovering, was currently onboard the D Star. In fact, I was going to make it my business, confront Nell about it, and get the whole sordid story out of her.

Just as soon as the effects wore off and her brain started working again.

I wish there was a nicer way to say this, but it was what it was, which I think is perhaps the only instance it appropriate to use that expression. It wasn't hard, either. Those little yellow pills – Percodan and aspirin – had become Nell's new best friend, so when I offered her a triple dose of yellow she actually tried to hug me. She didn't even ask me what the three purple pills were; just swallowed them down and tried hugging me again.

I told her it would make her sleep, which was true. I didn't exactly lie to her; I just didn't tell her the purple pills were Benadryl, which I knew from personal experience could put a meth addict to sleep for a whole day. She was out cold before we even arrived at Catalina Harbor.

Okay, I wasn't going to bore you with sailboat details, but whoever came up with the idea of making a sailboat with a transom that folds down deserves one of Lenny's Oscars. Imagine trying to offload a dozen gallon jugs of water and as many paper bags of groceries from a dinghy to a sailboat whose freeboard was four feet higher than you and whose transom didn't fold down. And as I did just that, easily and effortlessly at the stern of the D Star, I decided I would give the manufacturer a thumbs up on their website. They had earned it.

With the fold-down transom folded up, and two jugs of water in each hand, I made my first trip down the companionway steps towards the galley.

I was the only person onboard the D Star.

Chapter Thirty Six

The first thought was they had come for her, not even knowing who *they* were. So I started to panic because I couldn't imagine how, with all that dope in her, and the damage, she had just gotten up and walked away on her own.

Which was exactly what she had done, but only as far as the ship's head. Naked, laid out flat on her back, head resting on the teak slats in the shower stall, her body on the floor where the sink is. The bad foot was propped up between the toilet seat and the handle for the flush pump. Sound asleep and breathing noisily through the beat up nose and an open mouth. Probably should have checked the first aid book for side effects of mixing Percodan with Benadryl.

It wasn't worth disturbing her sleep to move her back to the aft cabin berth, so I tossed the blanket over her and left her in the head, then finished bringing the rest of the groceries down from the cockpit to the galley.

Twenty minutes later we were underway, me at the helm, my patient sleeping peacefully on the floor of the head. Our bearing was a little more than due south on a broad reach with the inflatable still inflated but trapped upside down on the foredeck by the self-tacking jib lines. The only thing I knew for sure is that we would eventually come within a couple miles of San Clemente Island on our port in about four hours; everything else was unsure. Thank god the weather was cooperating.

Remember all that planning that goes into a three day sailing trip? I was unprepared. All I had was a weather frequency on the radio, which told me to expect winds of about fifteen knots, building to twenty in the afternoon, with a two to four foot swell at nine seconds. Some sailing derelict from my past – not Redman – had once cautioned me to always double everything, just to be safe. So at least I was prepared for that: thirty knot winds and eight-foot seas every four seconds. Anything worse would probably come over the radio in time for me to react. Or not. Such a lack of readiness was unnerving; but considering my cargo, I had little choice.

* * *

That cargo woke up about four hours later with the pealing whine of an elongated version of my name. *Trippeeee! Triiip-eeee!* And like the indulgent, enabling caregiver I was, I dropped everything I was doing, which was nothing because the autopilot was doing everything, and came running.

"What the fuck?" she said to me, still on her back on the floor of the head.

"So, you're feeling better?"

"Why'd you move me?"

"In case you peed again," I lied. Otherwise I'd have to tell her about the Benadryl.

"I have to pee now," she said in that tiny voice damaged chameleons use to get what they want.

"I can help you with part of that. Then I think it's time to put some clothes on." Because she had managed to toss the blanket off and was once again buck naked, except for the bandages.

"Why? Don't you like what you see?"

"You are feeling better."

"I have to pee," she repeated as I helped her up from the floor and onto the toilet seat, which turned out to be an excruciating exercise for the girl, between the broken elbow, the hole in her side, and the mangled foot. "I think I'll use the cup from now on," she declared after the pain had subsided and she had caught her breath.

I turned around as she relieved herself.

"You're such a dork. All day you see me naked, and now you turn away."

"What color is it?"

"What?"

"The pee."

"Black, like oil."

I vowed never to mix Percodan and Benadryl again.

I found the best way to shut her up was by asking how she had arrived at her current physical state, because she was complaining about everything else, you know, that annoying type of whining that borders on endearing. She didn't want to be in the aft cabin anymore, but on the cushions of the main saloon. And she was hungry. And thirsty. And wanted more yellow and purple pills, which I realized might become my biggest problem; not that she was craving Benadryl, but that we might run out of Percodan before her pain stopped. It took me a minute to get the main saloon set up to accommodate her, which meant I had to leave her parked on the toilet seat, and believe me when I tell you that did not make the patient or her injuries happy at all, and she let me know it in explicit terms.

As soon as she was settled in, I told her it was time to check all the bandages, and you would have thought I was about to amputate something the way she complained. She refused ice for her face, which was the only part of her turning black, but I insisted we keep ice on the elbow because it might be broken.

"It's not broken," she said, agitated.

"But if it is, and we don't get it set--"

"It's *not*, I said." Spoken like a spoiled rotten chameleon.

I stopped all the fussing over her wounds and looked her straight in the puffy eyes. "What happened to you?" It came out sounding angry, which I was, but not at her so much.

She turned her head to the side and said nothing.

"Look at you. Beaten to a pulp and then pushed out of a car on the freeway."

No response.

"You're going to tell me, Nell. Or no more yellow pills." I had no intention of doing that, but I was desperate, and losing my patience.

She maintained her silence, and the thought crossed my mind that maybe she had been tortured for some piece of information she was holding, information she had refused to divulge, the consequence being her current physical condition. And here I was, threatening torture. Which made me feel like the perfect asshole.

Then I noticed the tears leaking out the side of one of the swollen eyes and realized I was an insensitive perfect asshole. I grabbed a roll of toilet paper from the head and gently dabbed at the tears running over her cheek before they reached the butterflied gash across her nose.

"You can throw me overboard, if you want," I said.

After a long pause the patient said, "I'm worried about Doug, Trippy," using the tiny helpless voice.

"Me, too. I don't know why he didn't come with us."

"I do," she said, her head still turned to the side.

When she said it that way, it was pretty easy to figure out why Doug wasn't on the boat. Because Nell was. He was protecting her.

She turned back to me. "No more questions?"

"No more." I patted what was left of the tears from her face. "Let me get some food ready." I stood up.

"It was a Rottweiler," she said, her face once again turned to the side.

"The dog? What was?"

"My foot."

I stayed quiet, having agreed to no more questions, despite having about thirty new ones based solely on what she had just told me. But a dog bite made sense. An organic meat shredder. It explained the nature and extent of the damage. I wanted to reexamine the injury, now that I knew what had caused it, but the timing sucked, so I let it go.

The ham and cheese sandwich on soft white bread, with its crust removed and cut up into what I figured would be manageable sizes for damaged lips, went uneaten; Nell was asleep again.

I decided not to wake her.

*   *   *

The D Star had managed herself admirably while I had been below with the patient, and had brought us alongside San Clemente Island. It's another long skinny stretch of isolated land, just like her sister, Catalina, maybe a tad more barren, considerably less friendly, due to her role as a secret US Navy base of some sort, but she would be the only company I'd have for the next three hours at our current course and speed which was still due south at just over six knots. I planned on keeping it that way as long as the wind permitted, for maybe another hundred miles, at which point, I'd have the option of hanging a left and heading straight for Ensenada, Mexico. Which was really my only option. Otherwise, our next landfall on this bearing would be Guadalupe Island in one and a half days of non-stop sailing, another stretch of barren land that was also some sort of secret military base, but for a different country.

I didn't own a satellite phone, and there was no internet or cellular this far out. In fact, the further south – and out to sea – we went, the less likely it was we'd have radio contact of any kind, unless it was from another boat in the vicinity. Which meant there was no way for Doug to communicate with us.

If Doug was still alive.

Three things clicked into my brain all at once, and together, they dictated the outline of a plan of action.

Assume Doug was alive – because I had assumed Nell was dead, and had been wrong.

Close to shore was the only place we'd have a chance of picking up a signal from Doug.

Stay in US waters, because the last thing I needed was the Mexican Coast Guard – which was really the Mexican navy – stumbling onto a foreign boat in their waters and discovering a battered woman in the care and custody of an ex-felon.

Chapter Thirty Seven

The message from Doug arrived on the fourth night in the form of a voicemail on my cell phone.

We had made it a routine over the past three days to sail in close to shore for periods of time, then bug back out to blue water, timing it so our coastal visits occurred at night, thus reducing the chances of being sighted, either by boat traffic along the coast, or by someone on shore, whoever that someone was. Nell was no help at all in that regard, refusing to discuss the details of the events that led up to her being pummeled. All she said – insisted, actually – was we do as Doug had instructed; otherwise both of our lives would be in danger, as well as Doug's. So I did what I was told, at least until I could get more information on what we were dealing with. Or who.

There were a total of three messages on my voicemail: two from Perry, hounding me about accommodating his clients' need to be healed, or whatever, and one from a prospective client, inquiring about pricing and availability. I had told Nell there was no word from Doug, and only casually mentioned the other three messages. She wanted to know the name of the prospect who had called, and when I told her it was some lady named Dorena, she asked me to play it. So seated in the main cabin settee, which, with the table folded down was now Nell's bed, I put the phone on speaker and replayed the message.

"Hi Trippy, my name is Dorena VanZant, I got your number from Jennifer in Bill's office. I was calling about setting up a charter. I don't know when yet. I guess that depends on the weather. Do you have anything available in the next two weeks? Anyway, give me a call when you can. I think I know what your rates are, but I'm wondering if you can accommodate a disabled person on your boat. Five-eight-two, seven-three five, eight-two-seven-three."

The message ended, and Nell said, "That was Doug." She didn't sound very excited about it.

"Who? The woman?"

Nell looked at me like I was an idiot, which maybe I was for asking that question. Then her expression clouded, and she said, "Dorena VanZant was his great-grandmother."

"Maybe a coincidence?" I asked.

"Nope."

Nell went silent. She started picking at a piece of the gauze wrapped around the bad foot.

"Well? What did he say? I mean she. Was it good news?"

"It was no news. Two more weeks. At least."

Nell quit picking at her foot and stretched out across the cushions of the bed. She propped the foot up on the back of the seats.

"Is that it?" I asked.

"Yep."

"What about all the other stuff, like the weather thing, and the disabled person?"

Nell raised her bad foot off the back of the settee and waved it toward me, but said nothing.

"You're the disabled person?"

"What do you think?"

Nell was shutting me out – again – this time to the point of being rude, and that irritated me. Our first contact with Doug, and her reaction was to sulk. You'd think I'd be used to it by now, being excluded from her thoughts. I guess I wasn't, and thought about saying something to her. Actually,

I thought about telling her she was being a bitch, but she wasn't, exactly, and didn't deserve the label anyway, at least not yet.

It amazed me that I didn't really know who this person was, the beat-up girl on my boat. Because it felt like we had been through a lot. Together. I thought I should know her. Deserved it, considering all that togetherness.

I was feeling entitled; I hate it when other people feel entitled. So I tried a different tack.

"Anything I can do to help?"

"If I think of anything, I'll let you know."

She didn't even look at me when she said that, which put her one step closer to bitch status in my mind. But I have a tendency to overreact in situations like this, so I waited a dutiful moment, then quietly headed back up to the cockpit.

Still feeling just a little entitled, considering I had saved Nell's life, and risked mine in the process, I worked the problem from the other side. God knows what the girl had on her mind, the pressure she was under, the dilemma that had led to a severe beating and the mess it no doubt left behind, a mess that presumably someone else was having to clean up for her, most likely Doug. And right now, she was stranded, on a boat in the middle of an ocean. With me. Nothing she could do about any of that. So I cut the girl some slack, because maybe she had that coming, maybe not. I just didn't know, and I guess that was the core of the problem.

The ocean is a strange and bewildering environment at night, frightening in its hidden potential, yet displaying a natural and alluring beauty that has enchanted mariners for centuries. Accordingly, alone in the cockpit on a windless night, I found myself gazing past the stern to an undulating blackness that felt both alien and familiar as it merged seamlessly into an explosion of brilliant stars. It was my own personal infinity, brimming with a sense of immediacy, and without my doing, the words *thank you* began chanting in my mind. What a strange and bewildering world we inhabit, and who was I to feel so entitled that it should all run as I expected it to.

"I know you think I'm a bitch."

I turned around to find Nell standing on the third step of the companionway stairs.

"Nah. I tried, but I've known too many genuine bitches in my life. You can wear bitch on your sleeve – like everyone else – but it's not in your heart. You don't mean it."

"My heart?"

Like that was presumptuous of me. "Maybe I should have said soul. Anyway, it's not there."

Nell remained silent.

"But you can still apologize, if you want," I continued.

"Do I strike you as that type of person?"

A funny thought occurred to me. I'd had this conversation before. With clients. Perry's clients. You know, the ones who think they're entitled to something just because of who they are. Or who everyone else thinks they are but they're not, really, and how all of that seems to come to a head when you're out in the middle of an ocean with no land in sight, because they know the truth, and now they're realizing that you know the truth, because reality in its simplest and most brutal form is all around them, and how that pops their bubble, suddenly robbing them of whatever power they thought they had over the world. And that thought answered her question for me.

"You strike me as someone who's got a lot going on right now and may have acted in a way that doesn't necessarily reflect your true nature. So, yes."

"I think you're just as stubborn as I am. When you want to be."

"I'll take that as a compliment."

"We're gonna run out of food and water."

"Not for another week. We'll hit the island again. Worked last time."

"What do you mean last time?"

"Where do you think we got all that ice?"

"When?"

"The first morning."

"Where was I?"

"Safe onboard. Sleeping, I guess."

Nell thought about this for a moment, and I wondered if I was about to get caught in a lie.

"Maybe," she said. "Depends on if they've made the boat."

"They?"

"You know, the ones who maybe aren't done trying to kill me."

"They're not trying to kill you. They just want something you have." Nell looked quickly to me, and I recognized the expression. "No, you weren't talking in your sleep. It's something I learned from Pete's people. Remember? The gang members you put me in business with? And your injuries. None of them fatal, but almost. Like torture. And those marks on your wrists. I'm guessing they were in the process of extracting something from you when Doug showed up and ruined all their plans. Up until then, they had plenty of time to kill you, but chose not to. Had to be a reason. Wanna talk about it?"

"Think about it, Trippy. If what you say is right, and despite all their efforts, I didn't talk, why would I spill my guts to you?"

"Because you trust me."

"That's true. But only because you have no idea what you're talking about."

"And you plan on keeping it that way."

Nell turned around and started hopping down the companionway steps using the grab rails for support. "I sure do."

She was somewhere down in the cabin, and I couldn't see her because all the lights were out. "By the way, I'm sorry. About being a bitch earlier."

"I'm gonna find out," I said loud enough to make sure she heard.

"You're gonna try."

Chapter Thirty Eight

Nell was seated in a corner of the cockpit, bad foot extended on the cockpit settee, organizing and rewrapping the tangled mess of static control lines piled on the seat and spilling onto the cockpit sole. She was using the hand with the bad elbow to hold the rope, the other one to form the coils. It was our seventh day at sea, a western wind offering us twelve knots across a cloudless sky, and her recovery had not presented any complications except for the foot, which would probably never be the same. Accordingly, I had granted her access to the cockpit, providing she behaved.

She was perhaps the worst patient in the world; accordingly, she was sick and tired of being pampered, a charge of which I was perhaps guilty. I had told her it was for her own good, which led to our first genuine confrontation – two days ago – wherein she announced it wasn't in her nature to lay around all fucking day doing nothing. So I told her to go sail the fucking boat for about six hours so I could get some sleep. I didn't mean it, of course, but was suffering from sleep deprivation. And of course she took it literally, and actually did take the helm, which actually worked for about three hours until she started messing with stuff up in the cockpit and accidentally disabled the autopilot. Which would not have been a problem if she had just maintained course, but when the sea unexpectedly grabbed the D Star's rudder and jerked the wheel out of her hands, it also yanked her bad elbow which caused her to flex the muscle group beneath the hole in her side. At least that's what she said happened. I figured the boat must have jibed in a decent amount of wind, and it was the noise of the boom's rigging slamming to leeward that had awakened me.

So we came to the agreement that she would help out wherever possible, providing the task did not exceed her capabilities. Of course, she couldn't leave it at that, and reminded me that if I had explained to her what everything in the cockpit does, the whole thing would have never happened in the first place, at which point I conceded, figuring it would be the most expedient compromise.

Day seven had started off considerably better. In fact, the harmonious atmosphere had encouraged me to press my luck. Which was why I was negotiating with her on the number of questions I could ask in regards her life, generally, and specifically, the incident which had led to her current physical state.

"Twenty questions," I said. "Just like the game."

"I'll give you three," said Nell.

"I deserve at least fifteen."

"Absolutely. I'll give you five."

I gave my nearly recovered patient a look as she coiled sail lines like she'd been doing it her entire life. She had just conceded two additional questions without much resistance, which I knew was out of character, and therefore suspected as a trap. Or ploy.

"So we agree to ten, then," I offered. "Ten questions."

"Actually, you can have all twenty." She was smiling, which revealed not only that she was up to something, but that the swelling in her face had diminished sufficiently to produce recognizable smiles. Both eyes were still blue-black, or the skin around them, but at least I could see those eyes, and I found that sexy in some perverse way.

Ok, you're right, I found everything about her sexy, in every way.

"What's the catch?" I asked.

"I get to redirect." She completed coiling the rope by passing a loop through its center and snugged it tight with the bitter end. "Every question you ask, I will answer yes or no, unless I can redirect it with a question. If I answer the question with a question, then your question doesn't count as a question, and my answer doesn't count at all. Naturally."

"Clearly your brain was damaged," I said.

"You'll get the hang of it. Go ahead; ask."

"Are you and Doug romantically involved?"

"Really? Of all the questions you could ask, you want to start there?"

"Yes," I said.

"One."

"What do you mean 'one'?"

"You just answered one of my questions with a 'yes'. That counts. You get a point. First one to twenty loses."

"But you didn't answer the question."

"No, you answered mine, which is the point, Trippy. Try again."

"The game could go on forever!"

"Not if you keep answering my questions."

I made a mental note to never again play twenty questions with a chameleon who thinks of everything and answers questions with questions.

"Besides," she continued, "that was a horrible question."

"How was that a horrible question?"

Okay, this one time I'll show you. Then you're on your own. Ask again."

"Are you and Doug romantically involved?"

"You mean currently?"

"Yes."

"Two. See why it was a horrible question?"

I smiled. "And if I answer *that* question, it would be three."

"Yep."

"One," I said.

"Told you you'd get the hang of it. Except technically yours wasn't a question."

Nell suddenly grimaced in pain. In our six days of bonded recovery, we had both discovered there were only three areas on her body that persisted in giving discomfort: the foot, the elbow, and the hole in her side, each of which was willing and ready to start hurting spontaneously without cause or reason.

"Which one?" I asked.

"Elbow."

"Want some ice?"

"Are we still playing the game?"

"Time out," I said. "Unwrap it so I can pack it."

I went below and chipped out some ice and put it in a plastic sandwich bag. When I returned to the cockpit, Nell had unwrapped the Ace bandage from her elbow which was still swollen, but nothing like it was on that first day. A yellow-black bruise had spread across the damaged area, fanning out both up and down the arm, and was now creeping around the front. I trapped the bag of ice in the bandage and started wrapping the arm again.

"You must have whacked it on something. Maybe you fell," I said.

"We used to be."

"What?"

"Me and Doug. It didn't work out. Or maybe it did. For the better, I mean. Doug's like the dream big brother. You know, being a girl in a man's world."

"And yet he left you."

"You would have done the same."

"Hardly."

"You're alike that way."

"Me?"

"You and Doug. Always thinking of the other person. To the point of exclusion. Like it just comes naturally to you. I'm not like that at all. I have to work at it. Kinda makes me jealous."

I finished wrapping the arm and used the same piece of tape that was already stuck on the end of the bandage to secure it.

"Twenty minutes with the ice," I said. "Then we'll pull it out."

Nell inspected my work, then looked me in the eye. "I'm dead because of Doug."

"You mean to everyone else out there. The bad guys, or maybe the good ones. The ones who hammered your elbow. Is that a good thing?"

"We playing the game?"

I smiled. "How about this: I ask you just one more question that I'm pretty sure you can answer with a simple yes or no without spilling your guts, and I'll concede defeat. Game over. You win."

"I like winning."

"No shit. Is that a yes?"

"I like saying yes to you, Trippy." It was that same look: putting me in a pot and cooking me.

"Don't go there."

"Why not?"

"Yes or no?"

Nell sighed. "Go ahead."

"Are you one of the good guys or one of the bad guys?"

Nell smiled, then leaned forward and whispered in my ear. "Make love to me and I'll tell you."

"Not on my list."

"Liar."

"You're wearing a pair of my jeans with a piece of jib halyard holding them up and a sweatshirt my sister gave me. It would feel like incest."

"Yes or no."

"Are you one of the good guys, Nell?"

Nell didn't like being turned down, not getting her way. Not that there are people who do, but it must have been bothering her that I was ignoring the chameleon, so she looked away from me, out towards the endless ocean vista, and made me wait a while.

"Where is it, Trippy?"

"Where's what?"

"That world you live in, where good people only do good things and bad people handle the rest, and it's effortless to tell the two apart." She looked back to me. "Show it to me. Take me there, because that's where I want to live."

"Pretty sure they wouldn't let you in. Something about honesty being a requirement."

"Of all the people to get stuck with on a boat in the middle of the ocean, I had to get Clark fucking Kent. With a felony and no superpowers. You shouldn't have made me out to be an angel in the first place."

"That's one thing I didn't do."

"Liar. All the women in your life start out as angels."

"You've known me how long?"

Nell adjusted the position of her arm with the ice pack on it. "Has it been twenty minutes yet? I'm taking it off."

"You'll regret it."

Nell half-laughed. "Regret and I share the same therapist." She was back to watching the limitless succession of waves. "How about you see me as the purest form of evil you can possibly imagine, and take it from there. That would be a good starting point. A safe one, at least." She turned back to look at me, to gauge my reaction to that last statement, but I guess she saw something else. "Don't go there."

"Where?"

"Looking at me like I'm some kind of angel. You've known me how long?"

"I don't know you at all. Which seems like a good starting point. A safe one, at least."

"Do you fall in love with every girl you meet?"

I leaned forward and kissed her gently on the lips. "Are we playing the game?"

And Nell returned the kiss while holding the arm whose elbow had a bag of ice wrapped around it.

Chapter Thirty Nine

You would have thought it was a scene from a sitcom, or maybe a romcom. It was hard enough for Nell just to get around with the bad foot. But going up and down the companionway steps required a gymnastics coach, you know, one of those spotters to catch her in case she fell. So it wasn't a pretty sight getting Nell down those steps while still making out with her, but it most likely would have made you laugh had you been there. Which I'm glad you weren't.

How do you define sex? Nell was so sore from all the damage somebody else had done to her body that I was hesitant to make any moves for fear of triggering one of those spontaneous pain moments, which would have dampened the mood. So we got as close as injury would permit to having sex, which probably was sex. I guess it depends on your point of view.

A few years ago I happened to be in the same room when the daughter of a friend of mine, attempting to explain her activities from the previous night, clarified to her parents that oral sex technically wasn't sex. I stayed quiet, naturally, partly because it wasn't my kid, but also because I happened to disagree. In fact the whole room got pretty quiet, considering the girl was still in high school. So depending on your point of view, or your definition of sex, Nell and I had a great time.

It got better. Imagine being at sea for ten days with someone who finds you sexually attractive, and nothing hopping on her good leg through the flooded cockpit until she reached the companionway.

At least she knew how to handle a sailboat.

She was also right about my problems just beginning.

Chapter Forty

It could have been a lot of things. Like the fact that we had spent every second of the past ten days together. Or that she was in some form of pain nearly all of the time. Or that she couldn't walk right. Or that we were dangerously close to running out of both food and water. But in my mind – and my heart – I knew it was the fact that I had just chosen information over love. Even that wasn't fair. I had told her, in no uncertain terms, that I was willing to say goodbye to her, in exchange for knowing what the hell she was really about.

Which I was taking as good news, honestly. If the girl wasn't interested, she would have pointed the boat home herself, and made up some story over the next hundred miles that I would have no way of checking, and then turned her back on me. Because she thought of everything and was good at what she did and answered questions with questions.

But it also occurred to me that Nell wanted it her way. She wanted to stay on the boat without ever telling me why or how she was involved in passing counterfeit plates to North Koreans via Southern California gang members. Or whether she was one of the good guys. Or how she managed to get a Rottweiler attached to her foot. In other words, she was using me. That's what the bad side of my brain was saying. I was dying to hear what the good side had to say about all of this.

She must have clipped the lame foot on something on her way below decks, because she was wrapping it in gauze and

I could see blood leaking through. She didn't look up, but said, "That was terribly unprofessional of me, and I apologize."

"Is that the kind of guy you get romantically involved with? The kind you can just push and shove until they fit neatly into a corner of your world? There when you need them, but out of the way the rest of the time? So in my mind, I made the right choice."

Nell said nothing as she wrapped her foot in the gauze, but at least she looked at me.

"Did you ever wonder why you and Doug make such a great team? No secrets, Nell. Or maybe you were just looking for someone to fuck for the next couple of months."

"Do you have any idea how stupid you're sounding right now? Not stupid dumb, but stupid ignorant."

"Ten days on a sailboat. You get to know the other person, no matter how little they say. I'm hardly ignorant when it comes to you. The real you."

She looked away. "You don't deserve the real me." She looked quickly back to me. "That came out wrong."

"Tell you what," I said, "we'll have this conversation when you're not feeling so sorry for yourself."

I turned and headed back towards the cockpit, mostly because I could hear the wind beating the shit out of the sails, but also because I wanted to make the point.

"So?" she asked before I was in the cockpit.

"So?" I answered.

"Where we going?"

"How about nowhere until you and I straighten things out."

She didn't have anything to say to that, so I returned to the cockpit.

The wind was building as it had been this time of the day for the past week, and the sails were taking the worst of it. I furled the jib, then released the main halyard and began the awkward task of lowering and flaking the mainsail to the boom in twenty-knot winds. At least I started flaking it in nice neat folds, but gave up because of the wind and concentrated on just getting the damned thing down. Which was when I saw Nell standing at the top of the companionway, shouting at me over the wind noise. I couldn't hear a word she was saying.

"Point her into the wind," I shouted back. "Then get the sail ties."

She ducked back into the cabin, then reappeared with the nylon ties used to secure the sail to the boom. On the good leg she hopped over to the starboard helm and cranked the wheel until the D Star stubbornly came to wind. After locking the wheel with the clamp, she joined me on the foredeck and handed me one of the ties. We each wrapped a sail tie around the crumpled mess of stiff Dacron and cinched our knots tight at about the same time.

"I asked you if you know who Richard Burr is?" said Nell.

"Should I?"

"He's a senator from North Carolina."

"Which is why I don't know him."

"He's also chairman of the SSCI. And you probably don't know what that is, either."

"You got me on that one."

"I've been to his house."

"Are you trying to get me to say something really mean and hurtful right now?"

"A coward would."

We were still standing on the foredeck, our arms draped over the boom, being buffeted by the winds. I looked to her sharply, because she was right about that last comment.

"Apology," I said.

"It complicates things, Trippy. The more you know about my past, the greater the chance it won't stay there. I need to keep things simple between you and me."

"I take it this is not the chameleon talking right now."

"No."

"Maybe I like you complicated. That's the only you I've ever known. Maybe I won't like the simpler version."

"You have so far. For the time we've been on the boat."

"But now we're talking about the future, aren't we?"

Nell said nothing.

"I don't mind keeping you off the radar, Nell, whatever the reason. Because I figured eventually I'd be dumping you and your problem back into the hands of Doug, and that would be the end of it. But you're talking about something else. A longer arrangement. Which means the problem stays here, on my boat, with you. And me. In the process of becoming us. And in that case, I think I deserve to know the reason."

Nell just stared at me, like maybe she was thinking about telling me everything, but I don't know. Maybe she was trying to figure out why her chameleon act was no longer working on me. At any rate, the conversation was officially over. Nell climbed off the foredeck and one-legged it into the cabin. I stood there for a minute, processing what had just happened, and what the implications were. It was that time, the time where I finally stood up and demanded to know everything about her, and what that meant for me and how it might affect us.

Otherwise she could walk home.

I went below.

She was seated on the edge of her makeshift bed, my phone in her hand.

"It's been arranged," she said.

"What has?"

"Doug will meet us in Morro Bay. The public docks there. Three days from now."

"You're not ready to go back yet," I said.

"You've left us no choice, Trippy."

"Us?"

"Don't bother," she said. "I can help. With the sailing, I mean. Six hour shifts, like we've been doing. We should make it there in two and a half days, plus time for complications."

"Poor choice of words," I said.

Nell started doing something with the cushions and the blankets and the pillows scattered on the bed, like straightening and arranging them.

"I don't get it."

"You're not supposed to." She stopped messing with the bedding and looked at me. "You want me to take the first shift?"

I grabbed a pillow out of her hand and threw it against the bulkhead. "Quit treating me like the mark. We're way beyond that."

"We're right in the middle of it, Trippy."

She was staying cool, like this was business, nothing personal. I stood directly in front of her. "Bullshit!" I yelled. I wanted to slap her, standing over her like that, and she must have sensed it, because her look was telling me to go ahead, daring me, because it would make her case, and ruin mine.

She waited a second, for me to do something stupid, but when I didn't she repeated herself. "So, you want me to take the first shift?"

"What if I say no? What if I point the boat due west until we hit Hawaii?"

Nell smiled coldly. "Well, for one, if you did that from our present position, you'd miss Hawaii by about a thousand miles, and two, you'd have to deal with Doug. And I think you already know Doug's the kind of guy who wouldn't stop until he found you. Or me, actually. His first priority would be me. Pretty sure he'd make you his second highest priority. For different reasons."

Whatever version of Nell I had just spent the last ten days getting to know had vanished. In her place was the mechanical version. Not the chameleon, not that cunning collection of variable charm that I had obviously and frequently confused with the genuine person, but something else entirely. Efficient, calculating, emotionless. Someone who was good at what they did, who thought of everything, and had decided answering questions with questions was a waste of time. And so were people like me.

And then I remembered the name you call people who act like this. "Now you're being a bitch," I said.

"Thank you."

She actually had the balls to smile at me after saying that.

In that very instant, because of the smile smeared across those lips, I was cutting my losses and moving on. It's an after effect of prison time. Something about suffering a total loss, and getting over it. It's always the first one that's the shocker. Being accused, being charged, being tried and convicted, and finding yourself in a nine-by-twelve cell for the next four years. With some other guy who also suffered that shock of total loss, but somehow got over it. After the first one, everything else becomes a manageable problem, no matter its severity. Shock, as an emotional reaction, loses some of its luster, its meaning. Its purpose. Getting over some girl who was spoiled rotten and feeling entitled and accustomed to throwing tantrums when she didn't get her way wouldn't be a problem at all.

The problem was I had raised my expectations over the past ten days on a boat with a girl I thought liked me. And once I realized that, it was pretty easy to lower them back to post-prison levels. Painful, but easy. Charged with emotion, but pretty simple to do. I didn't worry about the emotion part. That would go away, eventually, fade into the past and become mixed in with all the other failures and lessons learned and hard knock bullshit that was dangling behind me like a noisy, dirty tin can on a string tied to my leg.

Nell reached over to retrieve the pillow I had thrown and carefully placed it on the now orderly seat cushions. Like straightening things out in the cabin would make everything else okay. So I pretended, too, and opened up the laptop and started the navigation software. Something about the laptop made me think about my phone which Nell had left on the galley counter. I picked it up and looked at the messages. There weren't any. They had all been deleted, as had the entire call log. And the three voicemails, one of which had purportedly been from Doug. And all my contacts and saved pictures and all the other apps and programs that made smartphones smart. I had a useless chunk of plastic and metal in my hand. She had erased everything.

Of course she had.

Thinking of everything, and leaving no trace.

Which reminded me to keep my expectations at the lowest possible setting.

I refocused on the navigation software displayed on the laptop's screen, dropped a waypoint on the city of Morro Bay, and memorized the bearing.

"I got the first watch," I said to Nell, still pretending like everything was just fine, like I was okay with the way things had just worked themselves out. Then I headed topside, raised the main, unfurled the jib, settled into the cockpit and pointed the boat towards Morro Bay, another city on the coast of California, about halfway between Santa Barbara and San Francisco.

And honestly did my very best to focus on those things I could control. Which was sailing, and that was about it.

Chapter Forty One

We had been about ten miles west of Catalina when Nell had decided she didn't want to play with me anymore. So I kept the Channel Islands on our starboard side, maintained a westerly bearing, and gave Point Conception a wide berth of about thirty miles. Just over a day later we made a right and headed towards Morro Bay, which would take us another day or so.

It was some of the worst sailing I've ever experienced. A constant wind out of the northwest and a five-to-seven foot swell meant the D Star was averaging over six knots an hour, day and night, slicing through the ocean waves like a maiden on a mission, which she was. I know, that sounds like ideal sailing, and it was, but like they say about prison, it's not the time that'll drive you crazy, it's the people you have to do the time with. The sailing was great; the company was torture.

She wasn't being mean or anything, but she wasn't being nice, either. Like I said, mechanical, just going through the motions. She was polite enough, bringing me mugs of coffee and Styrofoam cups of noodles while I was at the helm, but she didn't mean it. Twelve days we'd spent alone together on the boat – laughing crying, yelling, kissing, sleeping – and in that time I had met three different versions of the same girl: the beaten Nell, the real Nell, and the other real Nell, who would never be beaten. At anything. By anyone. Which kind of summed up the whole issue, not knowing which one was the real Nell. Or worse, realizing the unbeatable Nell trumped all the others.

By design, and by nature, I suspect, love requires some dependency, and the thought forming in my head was that the unbeatable Nell was unconditionally independent. If you think of all the synonyms for love, like trust and sharing and confidence and compassion, those are all the things an unbeatable person might want to avoid, or have an aversion to. Incorporating those qualities into your life might just make you dependent. They can make you beatable.

So we didn't sit down and talk it all out. We didn't argue and shout and then make up and make love. In fact, we didn't talk at all, except when absolutely necessary. Like the food thing, because we decided to ration just to be on the safe side. Same with the water. So we'd discuss stuff like that, but there was no argument to it. Nothing but agreement which, of course is a really huge red flag that there's something funny with the relationship.

As in lack of spark.

No dependencies.

Unbeatable.

I know, I said I'd found a way to get over it, but you'd have to know the girl like I did to understand how difficult that was. Or still is. Okay, I only thought I knew her.

* * *

"I'm sorry things didn't work out, Trippy."

That's what she said to me after we had transited the breakwater coming in to Morro Bay. After we had spent two weeks on a boat, and had made love and shared meals and survived twenty knot winds. After I had nursed her back to health and taught her how to sail. That last part really bothered me. She was better because of me. I know, that's an incredibly egotistical statement to make, but I'm being honest here. How many times have I said doing the right thing always comes with consequences? Why should this time be any different.

"Yeah, me too," I had said, trying to make it sound like an upbeat downer, if there is such a thing, like we had planned a Fourth of July picnic and it ended up raining.

I had doused the sails before entering the channel into Morro Bay, so we were motoring at just under three knots, cruising along a quaint old seaside town made famous by a giant rock and ruined by the equally tall triple smoke stacks of a shoreline power station. Just my luck; Morro Bay's one of those romantic places where people tend to fall in love.

The sun was low in the western sky when we both saw Doug standing in the parking lot attached to the public docks. Nobody waved or anything like that. In fact, Doug just stood there, hands in the pockets of a windbreaker jacket, a beanie on his head. Nell got off the boat the way you'd expect someone to get off after spending two solid weeks onboard, the way I'd seen dozens of clients depart: in a hurry to walk on dry land. Before the D Star was even secured to the docks she had stepped off, still favoring the foot that had been bitten by a Rottweiler, and started a limp up the ramp towards the parking lot.

The departure was cold. Doug did not engage with her, or me. There were no embraces or waves goodbye. As soon as she was on the dock, he just turned around and headed toward the cars in the lot. Nell didn't look back, either. She just kept walking, along the dock, up the ramp, and onto the asphalt of the parking lot, and I followed her until her head disappeared into a row of cars.

That was the last time I saw her.

I thought about seeing if I could find a spot for the D Star in Morro Bay for the night, but after checking the food and water stores, I figured I had enough to last me to Santa Barbara, considering there was now only one mouth to feed. I hated Morro Bay all of a sudden, with all its romance and

charm and its ugly unfulfilled promise of hope. The ocean seemed like a fitting place for a guy like me. The middle of it.
　Alone.
　Peaceful.
　Quiet.
　Alone.

*　　　*　　　*

　I thought I saw her in Santa Barbara. That's where I did my retrofit, one full day after leaving Morro Bay, and it actually felt good to be on dry land. With the D Star tied in to a guest slip, I had checked in at a place called the Days Inn, which cost me nearly two hundred bucks, and was worth every nickel. It wasn't her, of course, coming out of some beaten down coffee shop that looked like it had been there for about a hundred years, but it was what I imagined she would look like, once she was out of the man's jeans and sweatshirt, and had had a shower. I saw her again in a car on Shoreline Drive, and a third time in the place where I bought groceries. It wasn't her, obviously. I just kept wishing it was.
　A day and a half wasn't nearly enough time to spend in Santa Barbara. I wanted to go to the intersection where supposedly I'd been involved in a traffic accident. And the hospital, I wanted to see that, too. But I realized I was chasing something that had never existed, despite the paperwork to the contrary onboard the D Star, so I loaded up the boat with enough food for maybe three more days of sailing, pumped diesel into the diesel tanks, garden-hosed water into the water tanks, and motored out of Santa Barbara with about four hundred less dollars than when I had arrived.
　Three days later, I was back in my home port of San Pedro. I figure I logged something close to four hundred hours of sailing over the past three weeks, so I called Perry, who was actually concerned, or at least as concerned as Perry

could get, and told him I needed a little time off before I started shuttling his tribe of weirdos around.

So I took a few days off and did nothing.

And then you guys called.

Bollis and Cleffler

Frank "Trippy" Deason pushed the two blown-up street photos of the persons who called themselves Doug and Nell back across the table until they were again in front of Bollis, which was where they had started over six hours ago when Deason had first sat down at the table with Bollis, and his partner, Cleffler. Bollis had loosened his tie and released the top button of his shirt since then, but now he was snugging everything back into place. Cleffler, meanwhile, had remained posted up in the corner of the room, just to the right of the two-way mirror, but was still giving Deason his signature deadman's stare, which Bollis doubted really worked, despite his partner's combination of cheaply crewcut hair and bushy eyebrows.

"That's it?" asked Cleffler.

"What do you mean?" said Deason.

"You dropped her off in Morro Bay and you never saw her again?"

"You make it sound like it's been years, and we were best friends," said Deason. "It's been less than a week. And I'm pretty sure I was the one who got dropped."

"Like they were done with you," said Bollis.

"She sure was." Deason fell silent for a moment and studied his hands, clasped in front of him on the wooden table. "All this time, I thought I was doing the right thing. Guess I didn't consider the consequences."

Cleffler shifted his stance off the wall and walked past the mirror and behind where Bollis was sitting, jabbing a finger into his partner's back as he passed by. So as soon as Cleffler was out the only door in the small room, Bollis stood up and told Deason he'd be back in a minute.

Cleffler was waiting for him on the other side of the door. He waited until Bollis closed the door, then they both moved over to the two-way mirror. Inside the room, Deason had spun the photo of Nell around so it was facing him and was staring at it.

Bollis said, "You don't believe him."

Cleffler sighed. "I don't know what to believe. Everything we've checked checks. Penny Page vouched for him, as did Jennison and Hayden. Both Haydens. And the Friedly lady. We're still waiting to hear back from the Coast Guard."

"You met Penny Page?"

Cleffler smiled. "Talked to her. On the phone."

"Did you ask her for your own private video?"

"Patel's the lucky one," said Cleffler.

"Why?"

"He interviewed the one Deason calls Jenny. In person. Who also corroborated his story. Or most of it, at least."

"No shit. Who is she, really?"

"Can't tell you."

Bollis looked at Cleffler like if anyone deserved to know it was him.

"No, I mean I can't tell you cuz Patel wouldn't tell me. But I got my suspicions."

Bollis waited. Cleffler made a poor imitation of a crow cawing and flapped his arms like they were wings.

"You're kidding me. That scene where she gets dunked in the vat of oil," said Bollis.

"Not hard to imagine her naked on a sailboat."

"What about the traffic accident, the guy that hit the Haydens?"

Cleffler smirked. "They didn't actually trade info. The guy took 'em out to dinner instead. Wined 'em and dined 'em. And then drove with them to the airport in some other car."

"What about a physical description?"

"Good luck. Male, Hispanic, dark hair, dark eyes, five-ten, about a hundred and sixty pounds, no marks, no tattoos. Go ahead and circulate that description and see what you get in the greater Los Angeles area."

"We could pull traffic surveillance footage."

"Of a guy matching that description. From maybe forty feet away. Shot in black and white at fifteen frames per second. At night. Unless he just happened to climb up one of the light poles and looked right into the camera for us."

Bollis said nothing.

"You'll never guess what his name was," said Cleffler.

"Who? The guy who hit the Haydens?"

Cleffler nodded. Bollis shrugged with his face.

"Pete Cardenas."

"Wait, wasn't that the dead guy they pulled--"

Cleffler raised his eyebrows.

Bollis smiled. "You gotta admit, Cleff, they're pretty good at what they do. Thinking of everything, like Deason said."

Cleffler gave Bollis the deadman stare. "I am so tempted to pull my service revolver out right now and shoot you in the head."

Bollis jerked his head towards Deason on the other side of the two-way. "So what do we do with him?"

Cleffler shrugged his shoulders. "He doesn't even know what a bitcoin is. Besides, you know how many patsies the department's interviewed just like this one? They all have a long and complicated story filled with a gazillion details that go nowhere. That's how these two operate."

"So we put a tail on him."

"Kinda hard to shadow a sailboat. And who's gonna pay for it? The Coast Guard? And for how long before nothing happens except somebody above our paygrade starts asking for the name of the idiot that decided we should put a tail on a sailboat. Besides, they're done with this guy."

Bollis thought about that.

"Tell you one thing," said Cleffler. "He's got the name right."

"Which one?"

"Chameleon."

The two men were quiet for a minute. They both looked back into the room and saw Deason spinning the picture of the girl around on the table. The guy's picture was turned face down. Then Bollis said, "You think she had it on her the whole time?"

Cleffler smirked. "Ones and zeros. That's what bitcoins are: cryptocurrency, a bunch of numbers. You could store half a billion in bitcoins on a flash drive, and still have room for a week's worth of porn."

"What, up her ass? For two weeks?"

"Maybe that hole in her side."

"Maybe she stashed it on the boat," said Bollis.

Bollis could hear Cleffler's cell phone vibrating in his pocket.

"Probably. But I doubt she left without it." Cleffler jerked his head towards Deason as he pulled his phone out. "Certainly not gonna leave it with him." He put the phone to his ear. "Yeah?"

He listened for a moment, then said "Okay," and put the phone back in his pocket. "The Santa Barbara thing checks out, too."

"The first time, or the second?"

"The second. Deason was there for a day and a half. Both the hotel and the marina. We already verified his first trip there. Police report, hospital records. It all checks out."

"Which he claims is all bogus," said Bollis.

"I hope not. Because that closes the loop. If they did manage to create and place phony police files, then these two got a lot more juice than we think. Which means they might actually be working for someone above our paygrade. Way above. But if that were the case, we wouldn't be interrogating this guy right now, because someone above our paygrade would have stepped in and put a stop to the whole thing. Which they haven't. But I agree with you; there's something missing from this picture."

"The bitcoins are missing," said Bollis.

"Besides that. Or maybe not. I don't know much about deep net cryptocurrency transactions, but two hundred fifty million is a lot of anything. Especially money, digital or otherwise."

"We could keep him overnight," said Bollis.

"We could keep him forever if it were a national security issue. Which it would be, if we could verify the whole counterfeiting thing. Which also closes the loop. For the same reason."

"Maybe we're the only ones not in the loop."

Cleffler looked to Deason through the two-way glass. "I don't think he's in the loop."

"I do," said Bollis. "I think he knows everything; he's just not talking."

"That's all he's been doing. And we got nothing."

"Back in the old days, we used to lean on 'em."

"Yeah."

"You know, rough 'em up a little, slap 'em around."

"Yeah."

"I miss those days."

"Yeah."

"Maybe we could--"

"Nah."

Cleffler's cell phone started buzzing again. He pulled it out and looked at the display. "That's not good," he said, then showed Bollis the number on the screen before answering it.

"Christ," said Bollis.

Cleffler put the phone to his ear. "Yes, sir." He listened for a moment then said, "Yes, sir," again. And then he said it a third time before disconnecting.

"Upstairs?" asked Bollis.

Cleffler sighed. "Yep."

"What do we do with him?"

"Nothing."

Upstairs

As Bollis entered the conference room, he wondered how anybody ever got anything done inside a room this high up with windows. He could see all the way to the ocean, and all the buildings and houses and liquor stores and perfect squares of green lawn and dots of people and streets and tiny cars stuck at stoplights in between.

He had been in this conference room before, but it was for some office party a few months back. Now there were men in the room, in suits that cost a lot more than his, and women in six-inch heels who weren't prostitutes but lawyers, probably. The oddball was the guy standing in the far corner of the room, at the window wall, looking out towards the ocean, like maybe he wasn't supposed to be here, but just wanted to check out the view from thirty-three stories up. He was wearing faded blue jeans and a starched white button-down dress shirt that wasn't tucked in. The shirt's cuffs were rolled halfway up the man's arms, and his hands were comfortably stuffed into his front pockets. Behind the man was an oak-brown credenza, and on top of it a black motorcycle helmet sitting next to a couple of glass pitchers filled with water. For some reason Bollis assumed the helmet went with the guy wearing jeans.

Bollis and Cleffler's direct report was a guy named Handelmett, and he was seated near the middle of the conference room table, facing the panoramic view. There were two empty seats next to him, and Bollis thought that was on purpose, so that he and Cleffler would be distracted by the view. Bollis took a seat first, thereby forcing Cleffler to sit next to Handelmett. Cleffler showed Bollis his teeth as he sat down.

Some guy Bollis had never seen before, seated on the same side as him, but towards the end of the table and wearing a dark blue suit with a yellow tie, started the meeting. Everyone was seated except the guy in jeans who was still standing at the window looking out towards the ocean.

"All right, ladies and gentlemen, since this is a mixed meeting, we're going to cover some areas that may already be familiar to some of you, so I ask that you bear with us. Andrea, would you like to start?"

Andrea was one of the women in high heels; her jewelry looked real. Had to be a lawyer, thought Bollis. She stood up.

"Well, I think we all know that two hundred fifty million bitcoin dollars were stolen from a Los Angeles Bitfinex office twenty-one days ago. And even that's misleading. It was one of their servers located at that site that experienced the theft; we're not sure yet, but we believe it was breached remotely, maybe from inside the office, but we haven't ruled out an external ingress."

"Excuse me, a what?" said some other guy Bollis didn't recognize, seated a couple chairs down from Andrea.

"Wireless. They could have been outside the office. Maybe in the hallway, maybe the building's parking lot. We're working on that," said Andrea.

Bollis corrected his previous assumption. Not legal; she was IT or something.

"What we are sure of," continued Andrea, "is that the ident and access authorization package used to negotiate the fund transfer belonged to a Russian investment bank, Renaissance Capital. One of the encryption nodes confirmed at least that much."

Bollis tried to stay focused, but encryption nodes, and whatever they did, were above his paygrade. He started counting the number of city blocks between the ocean and this building, and was on twelve, when something else the IT woman said refocused his attention.

"...a dead end transfer, which means the bitcoins didn't go from one place to another, like from bank to bank, but rather to a device, most likely a remote drive of some sort. Which in itself, is not against the law, but is usually the first step. Which is why the Treasury department got involved."

Not IT, thought Bollis. More like an accountant or something, for the US Treasury. Or maybe the SEC. Then he started thinking about where on her body the girl called Nell would have hidden a thumb drive.

"Naturally, we questioned Renaissance Capital about the transaction, which was when it was reported as a theft," said Andrea.

"Somebody from within Renaissance Capital stole it from their own company?" asked one of the other women seated at the table.

"Renaissance Capital maintains the bitcoin transfer was a planned financial transaction which was then intercepted by another as of yet unidentified team," said Andrea. "But I think Agent Lee is better suited to answer that question."

"What about the person of interest downstairs," interrupted the guy in jeans. He was still facing the windows. No one objected to the interruption, which told Bollis the guy belonged here.

Handelmett looked to Cleffler who looked to Bollis, then back to Handelmett, who nodded to Cleffler.

Cleffler said, "He spent the last two weeks with the female suspect. We've been able to verify most of his story but--"

"Suspect?" asked the man in jeans, without looking at the room.

"The Russians believe she and her male partner were the sources of the interception, and therefore responsible for the theft. The unidentified team."

"Which Russians? Government officials?"

"Sorry, Renaissance. Their security division. Initially they were able to detain her, but somehow she was able to escape custody."

"And your person of interest downstairs played a role in said escape?" asked the man at the window.

"Not directly. Not that we know of yet."

"Have you successfully connected him to the wireless interception and subsequent theft?"

Handelmett was looking uncomfortable. "We believe he interacted directly with the suspect immediately after she came into possession of the transfer."

"So Renaissance Capital admits to negotiating the transfer, onto a remote medium, for some unknown but business-related reason, then claims that medium was intercepted by unknown persons, whom they detained but unsuccessfully, whom they are now labeling as suspects," said the man still looking out the window. "And the person of interest now detained downstairs has no direct relation to either the initial theft or subsequent escape of the alleged suspect?"

"We are in the process of determining that," said Cleffler. "He's still just a person of interest, at this point."

"Has he been cooperative?" asked the man in jeans.

"Yes."

"And you've verified his story?"

"So far."

"How did you come across this person of interest?"

"The Russians' security team suggested him as a possible accessory," said Cleffler.

"You mean Renaissance."

"Yes."

The room went silent, and Bollis found it funny the way everyone was deferring to the guy in jeans, hesitant to interrupt his thinking process, maybe even afraid to. Bollis wondered how important you had to be to get away with wearing jeans to a meeting where everyone else was in suits and high heels.

"Mr. Handelmett," said the guy in jeans, who still hadn't turned around to face the people he was talking to, "I wonder if you can shed some light on the logic here. Your team is following up on a lead supplied by the persons we know to be the last ones in possession of the stolen funds – Renaissance – who claim there was another involved party, of which no one can attest, except the persons we know to be the last ones in possession of the stolen funds."

The man finally turned away from the windows and looked directly at Handelmett. "They have you chasing after a set of persons they want you to believe are responsible for the theft. They even provided you with a material witness that suggests the evidence points to said set of persons." The guy in jeans waited a moment then said, "I want you to believe that also fits the profile of a red herring."

Every set of eyes in the room was now focused on Handelmett. The jeans guy turned back to the window view and continued. "My guess would be the person you have downstairs is a plant, a gift from Renaissance, whose sole purpose is to misinform, mislead, and obfuscate. Have you performed a background on him? Is he of Russian descent? An upstanding member of our community? Any brushes with the law? Who did he vote for, last election? How much money does he have in his bank account? Any recent unusual financial transactions?"

It was so quiet in the room Bollis could hear the whoosh of the building's HVAC system as it pumped conditioned air in and out of the conference room through vents in the ceiling. Handelmett and Cleffler were whispering to each other. Bollis couldn't hear what they were saying, but he knew Cleffler was now telling Handelmett that the guy downstairs was an ex-felon with a bunch of stock in Google, and a two hundred thousand dollar sailboat he couldn't afford. Then he saw Handelmett's expression wrinkle up, like anyone's would when a piece of vital information was unexpectedly dropped in their lap.

"We are in the process of building his profile as we speak," Handelmett finally said to the room. It sounded weak, thought Bollis, and he wondered if everyone in the room could see how red his face was.

"A solid lead if there ever was one," said the main wearing jeans, but Bollis could tell he hadn't meant it like it sounded.

"Can anyone in this room educate me on the significance of a two hundred fifty million dollar bitcoin theft?" continued the man dressed in jeans. "I mean generally. How does the market react to such an event?"

No one said anything right away, so a woman seated two chairs left of Bollis said, "The Bitfinex market dropped thirteen percent on the day of the incident. But within two business days it had fully recovered."

The man wearing jeans spun around and looked to the woman. "Do fluctuations like that present an opportunity within the market environment?"

"Of course," said the woman, "But you'd have to know it was coming to take advantage of something like that."

And as soon as she had said those words, everyone in the room had the exact same thought. Bollis could see it on their faces: a dawning, and in this case, embarrassing realization. Christ, even Bollis could do the math: this wasn't about the theft of bitcoins; it was about manipulating financial markets.

And just like that, everyone in the room was suddenly talking at once; to each other, on their phones, rectangular black earpieces with blue lights blinking. People were standing then sitting down then standing again, walking back and forth, sifting through papers on the table, shaking and pointing fingers at each other. It was chaos. Bollis heard terms being thrown out like 'pump and dump', and 'arbitrage' and 'market spikes' and 'short selling', and then he realized Handelmett was talking to both Cleffler and himself.

"…You two wanna fuck me, you sure picked the perfect time to do it. Two hours I want that shit on my desk! Goddamn it!"

Cleffler was stupid enough to ask Handelmett what they should do with Deason.

"Do you not understand what just happened? Forget about him. And everything he told you. It's all bullshit. Made up. Refocus on Renaissance. Now!"

It was the second angriest Bollis had ever seen his boss, and he could care less; he was three years and seven months away from retirement. Fuck Handelmett, he thought. Bollis then looked over to the guy that had started all the ruckus and realized the man dressed in jeans and an untucked dress shirt was no longer in the conference room.

Neither was the motorcycle helmet.

Cisco Kid

Seven fucking hours, thought Trippy Deason. In a tiny room with a two-way mirror. Nell had not said anything about it taking that long, but there wasn't much he could do about that now. He was just glad to be out of there. *Seven fucking hours!*

It had been the truth, he told himself. Almost all of it. Every part of it, in fact, right up to the very end. They just hadn't asked him if she had said anything else, if the two of them had made other arrangements. Maybe they would have gotten around to that, if they hadn't let him go, which meant Trippy would have lied even more. It was a matter of trust; he had decided a long time ago to mistrust law enforcement. Now he was wondering if placing that same trust in the same people who had shot him in the chest – and drugged him, and sank his boat – really was the safer alternative.

He wondered if he was doing the right thing.

And about the consequences that would be coming. Because that was the only thing he could trust: there would be consequences.

The building's elevator dumped him into the subterranean parking lot where he had parked the Rabbit. After wandering around for a whole two minutes, because everything looked the same down there, Trippy finally found his car, parked in a place he didn't remember parking in. He let himself into the car and closed the door. He checked the time on his watch, and then he checked his phone. It had been dead ever since Nell did whatever she did to it – no calls, no messages, nothing – and yet here he was, waiting for a text message. There was no point in going anywhere, because he didn't know where to go. Don't go anywhere until the message arrives, Nell had told him. Then he wondered if it was a good idea to hang around in the building, or under it, right underneath their noses like this. Something could go wrong. Because as usual, Trippy didn't know the whole plan, just his part in it. Trust issues.

The people who had shot him.

And sank his boat.

Maybe this was the final screw, where he voluntarily walks into the federal building or whatever it was, spills his guts about everything that had happened over the past several months of his life – about trafficking counterfeit plates and people dying and keeping some girl off the radar after she had been beaten up because she had probably committed some crime involving something called bitcoins – and in doing so, had implicated himself to the point where, if they couldn't find the ones who had done whatever crime had been committed, they'd just grab whoever they could and pin it on that guy, which was Frank "Trippy" Deason. Because he had walked in there voluntarily and spilled his guts. Because that's the way justice worked unfortunately; he knew that from personal experience.

Meanwhile Doug and Nell would be in another city, or state, or country by now. It had been her idea to cooperate, to make a statement to the cops or the feds or whoever those two guys were. Just like getting shot had been their idea.

The final screw.

And the consequences that were bound to come with it.

Another prison term.

For something he hadn't done.

Again.

All because he had fallen in love with a perfect stranger.
Who happened to be a chameleon.

His phone started vibrating. And then ringing. And then beeping like it had just received a text message. Then it clunked three times like it did when the battery was low. Trippy picked the phone up from the passenger seat and saw there was a map on the display, and a pop-up box with an address in it, with one of those virtual stick pins stuck into a point on the map. It was a city block, but the scale was so small, he couldn't tell what part of the city the map was showing him. He pinched the image with his fingers to shrink it down, and the display went black. The phone was dead again. He was about to throw the phone when it said in a mechanical female voice, "Take Third Street to the 110 freeway." It kept repeating those directions, like every other second, until Trippy managed to get the car started and was backing out. Only then did the phone shut up.

The subterranean parking lot exited onto Figueroa in downtown LA, and Trippy could see the lights and cars of the freeway ahead by a couple blocks, running parallel to the street in front of him. He made a right onto Figueroa, and the phone started squawking, "Go west on Figueroa to Third Street." So he made a U-turn on Figueroa and started heading the other direction, and that seemed to make the phone happy. Two short blocks later, he saw Third Street, and made a right. The phone said nothing. A minute and a half later, he was on the 110 freeway heading south. The phone remained quiet. Trippy put the phone in his lap.

It was just past seven in the evening, which meant freeway traffic was heavy but moving at a moderate pace. Trippy chose the middle lane of the freeway, because he didn't know what was coming next, and split his attention between the road and the phone, in case it had something else to say, or the map image came back. It remained blank and silent. After twenty silent minutes going south on the 110, the phone came back to life, directing him to turn east on

Anaheim Street, and Trippy knew exactly where he was – in the city of Wilmington, about two miles from where the D Star was slipped.

The surprise came when the phone's voice told him to turn off of Anaheim onto a street called McDonald, a residential block crowded with tiny houses that had been built nearly a hundred years ago by some guy who had made a fortune in chewing gum. The street itself was packed with parked cars, all of them vintage Chevys and Cadillacs and Lincolns and Buicks dating to the fifties and sixties, less than six inches off the ground, tricked out with oversized spoked wheels, polished chrome and elaborate paint jobs that probably cost as much as the car itself.

Lowriders.

Like a car show, maybe half a million dollars' worth right there on a street in a questionable area of Wilmington, eight o'clock on a Wednesday night. Except there were no people to go with the show. No drivers or spectators or bystanders. No one. The entire block was lifeless.

Which was when Trippy began thinking something was up.

"You have arrived at your destination," said the digital female inside his phone.

The digital map reappeared on the phone with an address and a google picture of the house, taken during the day. Which was of no help to Trippy, considering it was night.

The actual house still stuck out from the rest of the neighborhood because it was the only place with no lights on, inside or out. In fact, it looked vacant. Trippy looked for a place to park which was when he realized the only place to park was directly in front of the house in question on the other side of the street. He pulled in behind a motorcycle that had been parked perpendicular to the street, and nearly touching a glistening black 1960's Chevy Impala whose body was actually resting on the pavement. He killed the car's engine and waited. The phone was stuck showing the picture of the house with its address in a pop-up box.

Fifteen minutes later Trippy had not moved from his car, and absolutely nothing had happened. No sign of life from the darkened house, no nosy neighbors peering through curtains, no ambient music drifting over the night air, no other cars driving down the street. Just dead silence. The phone had blanked out again, and was just as quiet as everything else.

The knock on the passenger side window made him jump in his seat. It was a gang member wearing a blue bandana wrapped around his head, another one tied across his face, and a pair of wraparound sunglasses concealing his eyes. Trippy fumbled to find the button to roll down the passenger side window when he noticed the other gang member standing just outside his door.

It was the guy with the beanie. Trippy lowered the driver side window.

"Good evening, Mr. Deason. We're very glad that you were able to make it. May I invite you inside? We have some refreshments waiting for you."

"I was beginning to think I had the wrong place," said Trippy as he exited the car, because he didn't know what else to say.

"I apologize for the delay, but we had to make sure you weren't followed," said the guy with the beanie.

Trippy hadn't thought of that, and out of reflex he looked down both directions of the street.

"Don't worry," said the guy with the beanie. "No one comes here unless they're invited. May I have your keys, please?"

"My keys?"

"To your car."

Trippy handed over his keys to the guy with the beanie who said something in Spanish as he threw them back to the bandana guy still standing by the Rabbit.

"And your phone."

Trippy gave his phone to the guy with the beanie who dropped it into the front pocket of his baggy pants. They began walking towards the front door of the house.

There were at least forty people crowded into the living room of the small house, nearly all of them dressed in baggy blue jeans and white tank tops, and wearing blue bandanas across their faces and on their heads. Candles were the only source of light; dozens of them, lined up across the mantelpiece of a fireplace and clustered in groups on small tables about the room, their light diffused by stagnant clouds of smoke. The furniture looked old, like maybe it had been there since the house was built. There were gang members piled onto a couch, women on the laps of men, other men seated on the arms of the sagging couch. The place smelled of cigarettes, marijuana, stale beer, and cinnamon, an aroma Trippy suspected was coming from the candles. A song he had not heard in years was playing from somewhere, perhaps deeper into the house: *The Cisco Kid*, performed by War. This was a party. Of gang members. Wearing blue bandanas across their faces that they would pull down in order to drink the beer from a bottle.

An unmasked member walked up to Trippy and offered him a bottle of beer. It was the same guy who had accompanied beanie guy the last time they had met, aboard the D Star – his right hand man, the flashlight guy.

Trippy accepted the beer and said thank you. The flashlight guy said, "Good to see you again, Mr. Deason."

"Likewise."

As the flashlight guy receded back into the crowd of anonymous blue bandanas, Trippy watched as his host – the guy with the beanie – crossed the living room and approached a man who clearly did not belong in the room. It was a white guy with dark, close-cropped hair, about the same age as Trippy, dressed in faded jeans that actually fit, and a white, button-down dress shirt that was untucked. The two shook hands, and then the guy with the beanie handed the man Trippy's phone.

"What are you doing here?"

It was a girl standing to Trippy's right, dressed in a white sports jersey with the number thirteen on the front of it. No bandanas or glasses hiding her face, so he could see she was smiling at him.

"He's our guest," said the guy with the beanie who was suddenly back at Trippy's side. Trippy looked over to where the guy who had his phone had been standing. He was gone. Of course.

The girl in the jersey took a long look at Trippy, then smiled again and said, "I hope you enjoy yourself, Mr. Guest." Then she, too, merged back into the crowd.

The guy with the beanie said, "I'd like to introduce you to someone."

The guy with the beanie started weaving his way through the crowd and Trippy followed. They walked through a cramped kitchen painted years ago in yellow, down a dark hallway crowded with gang members to a bedroom door. The guy with the beanie opened the door and gestured for Trippy to enter.

There was no furniture in the room except for a six-foot floor lamp shoved into a corner, its shade missing, and a single incandescent lightbulb doing all the work.

There were two people in the room.

Doug was one of them.

A Search for Truth

Doug's face lit up when he saw Trippy. He took three giant steps across the small room and threw his arms around him into a bear hug, like old college buddies reuniting.

"Trippy!" said Doug, as he actually lifted Trippy off his feet. Doug broke the embrace, but kept his hands on Trippy's shoulders. "Look at you! You look great! Didn't I tell you the vest would work? Good as new!"

"You don't look too bad yourself, considering the last time I saw you."

Doug got serious and said, "You did an awesome job, Trippy. We'll never be able to repay you."

"We?" said Trippy.

Doug turned to the other man in the room and said, "A single shot to the chest at five hundred thirty yards. The vest worked."

It was the man in jeans and the untucked shirt, the guy who had Trippy's phone.

"Trippy," started Doug. "This is a friend of mine. Bill, meet Trippy."

The man named Bill stuck a hand out, and as Trippy shook it, the man used his other hand to cover the handshake. "I've heard a lot about you, Trippy."

"All of it good, I hope."

"We wouldn't be meeting if it weren't."

"You work with Doug?"

"Yes."

"And Nell?"

Doug and Bill shared a look.

Doug said, "We'll get to that in a minute."

Trippy didn't like the way that sounded, and was about to say something when Bill handed Trippy his cell phone.

"I believe this is yours."

Trippy took the phone. "Yeah, but it doesn't work." He looked to Doug. "Your partner did something to it."

"All fixed," said Doug. He was smiling.

Trippy looked to the phone. Everything was back to normal. Even his list of contacts had been restored.

"How's the boat?" asked Bill.

Trippy alternated his look between Doug and the new guy. And then he just made up his mind that now was the time. Because there might not be another time. In fact, he knew, somehow, there would never be another time after now.

"Are you guys ever going to tell me what this was all about?"

Doug said no at the same time that Bill said yes. Doug shrugged his shoulders.

"What do you want to know?" said Bill.

Trippy got stuck. Because there were so many questions that had built up in his mind over the past few months he didn't even know where to begin.

"The counterfeit plates," Trippy said.

"What about 'em?" said Bill.

"Why were you passing them to the North Koreans?"

"I can't tell you that. National security."

"So you work for the government."

"Absolutely not."

"Then it's not national security."

"It is," said Bill. "Next question."

"Who beat Nell up?"

"Let's just say it was the Russian mafia," said Bill.

"Why can't we say who it really was?"

"It was the Russian mafia."

Trippy looked to Doug. "You, too?"

Doug nodded.

"Why?"

"Because she stole something that belonged to them," said Bill.

"Why?"

"Because I told her to."

"So you're the reason she got beat up."

"I guess you could say that."

"I don't want you to guess. I want you to know."

"All right, yes, I'm the reason she got beat up."

"Why would you do that?"

"Two hundred fifty million in bitcoins, that's why."

"I don't even know what that is," said Trippy.

"I know," said Bill.

"That's why we trusted you to bring it to us here tonight," said Doug.

"I didn't bring you guys anything."

Doug looked to the phone Trippy was still holding in his hand.

Doug said, "Nell transferred the stolen bitcoins from a flash drive to your phone. While you guys were on the boat. Which was why we gave your name to the Department of Justice. So they'd interview you. Also why your phone wasn't working. She locked it. Works now, though."

Doug had explained it like it was as simple as renewing your driver's license, while Trippy was wrestling with the concept of good and evil. Or the definition. Right and wrong. Or that fine line between the two. And how he may have been the one that had just blurred that line. Towards the evil wrong side. It seemed there were consequences no matter what he did, right or wrong. Or how he did it. Or how it was done to him.

"So I helped you guys steal two hundred and fifty million dollars."

"From the Russian mafia, Trippy. Not sure that counts as stealing," said Doug.

"That's not how they see it."

"It was a recovery operation," said Bill. It sounded like he was getting impatient. "Look, Trippy, I appreciate all of your help up to this point but--"

"Where's Nell?" Trippy demanded.

Doug and Bill shared another look. Bill looked down to his hands, then half turned away. The room was silent except for the muffled bass of music coming from somewhere else in the house, and Trippy realized it was the same song that had been playing when he first entered the house: *Cisco Kid*. In fact, he realized the song hadn't stopped playing since he'd been in the house.

"That was the deal," said Trippy. "I show up, Nell leaves with me."

"We're not the ones who broke the deal, Trippy," said Doug.

"What's that supposed to mean?"

Now Doug was looking down at the floor, like he didn't want to look Trippy in the eye, didn't want to be the one to tell him that Nell really was one of the bad guys. *The chameleon. The fucking Chameleon. She's the one who broke the deal, stupid.* And then it occurred to him that maybe the news was even worse than that.

"What happened?" asked Trippy.

"We don't know," said Doug.

"What does that mean?"

"Where she is. We don't know where she is," said Doug.

"How can you not know? You were with her. In Morro Bay. I saw you. With her. I delivered her to you. She got into a car with you. She was with you! You were the last one with her!!" Trippy had shouted that last statement, and now the door to the room was opening. The guy with the beanie stood in the doorway. Doug waved him off. The beanie paused a moment, looked at Trippy, then to Bill and Doug, then retreated, closing the door.

"I lost her," Doug said. "In Santa Barbara. We were working our way down the coast, you know, taking our time, low profile, all that. But Nell wanted to stop in Santa Barbara, so we did." Doug looked back down to the floor. "She ditched me in a coffee shop. Went to use the bathroom and never came out."

"That makes no sense at all," said Trippy.

"Actually, it does," said Bill. He looked to Doug. "You two should have stayed separated. It was too soon. Possibly three agencies looking for you. And the Russians. Something spooked her. She was following procedure. It makes perfect sense."

"They grabbed her. The Russians," said Trippy.

"Unlikely," said Bill. "Couldn't have tracked her. Not after the boat."

"Well someone did," said Trippy, like he was angry, because he was.

The room went quiet again. *Cisco Kid* was still playing.

"Nell thought we were being followed," said Doug.

"God damn it!" said Bill. "When were you going to tell me that?"

"Maybe it was the cops," Trippy said.

"It wasn't. We'd know about it," said Bill. "But the fact of the matter is we don't know anything." Bill looked to Doug. "And you know that doesn't sit with me very well."

Doug was back to looking at the floor.

Bill said to Doug, "You need to fix this."

"I know. And you know I always do."

"What do you care," said Trippy to Bill. "You got what you wanted."

Bill gave Trippy a look, like maybe he had overstepped with that last comment. Then he looked to Doug, like maybe this was all Doug's fault because he was the one who got this bozo caught up in the mess to begin with. Then Bill smiled tightly and stuck his hand out to Trippy.

"This will likely be the last time we meet. I'd just like to say thanks."

Trippy hesitated but shook the hand, and just as abruptly Bill was heading for the door. He opened it and stopped to say something to the guy with the beanie who apparently had been standing guard on the other side the whole time. Then they shook hands and Bill left.

Doug said, "I'm sorry, Trippy. You know how I feel about her. I would never let anything happen to her."

"You failed, Doug. You failed."

It was a horrible thing to say, especially to Doug. But Trippy left it that way, and walked out of the room, leaving Doug alone in the room.

Out in the hallway, Trippy said to the guy with the beanie, "I'd like to leave now, if that's okay with you."

"What about your friend?" asked the guy with the beanie.

"You mean the girl. Nell. She couldn't make it."

"I'm very sorry to hear that, Mr. Deason."

"Yeah, me too."

"You know, my mother used to always tell me that things happen for a reason. And you know what? Most of the time she was right." The guy with the beanie smiled, then offered his hand. Trippy accepted the handshake and returned the smile.

"I don't even know your name," said Trippy.

"My mother named me Cesar, but your friend calls me Playboy."

"Playboy. Is that a compliment?"

"It is coming from her."

The guy with the beanie, whose proper name was Cesar, raised his eyebrows and smiled. So did Trippy.

"If there's ever anything you need, Mr. Deason, I hope you will feel free to call upon me."

"I will." Trippy started to leave, then turned back to Cesar. "You know, that same song's been playing ever since I got here. Cisco Kid, by War."

Cesar raised his eyebrows again. "Do you like it?"

"Yes, I do, but…the same song…"

Cesar then reached into his pocket and pulled out a small flash drive. He handed it to Trippy. "War's greatest hits. A gift for you."

"For what?"

"A reminder, Mr. Deason. Of our time spent together." Cesar smiled. "Maybe you can listen to it while sailing that boat of yours."

Trippy smiled back. "Thank you, Cesar."

"No, thank *you*, Mr. Deason, thank *you*."

Distraction

It was a short drive from the house in Wilmington to the marina, and Trippy didn't remember any of it. It had seemed so genuine when she said she'd be there, so definite, so committed, like it was from the heart, from one heart to another. Like they had meant something to each other. She had even made a point of saying this wasn't a chameleon promise, but a real one. One he could count on. They had sealed it with a kiss. And more. It was why he had agreed to the rest of it, why he had let her go in the first place, and why he had lied to a couple of guys in suits in a room asking questions.

Because it was nothing like he had told them. At least not at the end. Trippy had relented; he would let Nell stay with him, and he would never again ask questions about her past. Or her future. Because she wanted to retire, and he wanted to be with her. They would focus only on the now. They had agreed to that, and then they had made love, for three days straight, in the cockpit, letting the autopilot do all the work as it carried them towards Morro Bay.

There would be consequences for her actions, on her end, maybe on his end, too, and they had discussed that as best as they could, considering what little information she had chosen to share with Trippy. There was Doug to think of, and the person she and Doug worked with – or for, she later clarified. They agreed that Doug would be a problem – a good problem, but one nevertheless. But Nell was confident there was a way, and Trippy was to leave that to her. She couldn't bear to lie to Doug, but it seemed the most likely path. The easiest, at least. It would be done her way, she kept repeating, and Trippy would not be privy to that way. He was allowed no opinion in the matter. She had asked him to trust her, and he had said of course. Because she had been good at what she did and would think of everything, like she always did. Because he was in love with her, and no longer cared if that would ever become just plain love; *in* love was a good start, a *now* start. It was a state of being that captured the essence of the now moment. And that's where they had agreed to live, together, for now.

She had said it would be wrong, her plan, and painful, and it would hurt some people, and it would finally define her as one of the bad guys, at least in the hurt people's eyes, and Trippy was okay with that, too. Because that was then and this was now, and whatever Nell's plan, its point, its purpose was to preserve and prolong the now. So they had agreed to the plan, and its consequences, each of them for their own selfish reasons.

And then they had returned to making love.

So all of that was how and why Trippy knew that something had gone horribly, unexpectedly, and disastrously wrong. Because he hadn't made the agreement with the chameleon; he had made it with the girl on his boat, whoever that was, the *real* whoever, the *real* it didn't matter who she was, the version of Nell who absolutely would not stand him up. The unbeatable Nell.

So it had to be for another reason. Something else had come up, had gone wrong. Maybe the Russians or the guys in suits or something else entirely. Something the girl who thought of everything hadn't thought of, hadn't anticipated, hadn't planned for. Even Doug didn't know where she was, and Trippy wondered if that was a first, or whether it was a lie. He always knew where Nell was, always, looking after her, putting his life in front of hers, keeping her safe. And just like that, Trippy was feeling like shit for not saying more to Doug. Or less. For not telling him it would be okay, and that she'd show up, somewhere, and that she could take care of herself in the meanwhile, because they had made a deal, the two of them, Trippy and Nell, an arrangement. And he was sorry if it hurt Doug, but they both had to trust Nell knew what she was doing.

But he hadn't said any of that

He'd been a jerk instead.

The marina parking lot was deserted, which was normal for a Wednesday night at ten o'clock. Just a handful of cars, some of them covered, others dusty from lack of movement, some broken down and incapable of movement. But for the first time it was feeling like a lonely place, a place where things end sadly, or never get started to begin with. Trippy parked and killed the Rabbit's engine and after sitting there, alone, in the driver seat, waiting for nothing, attempting to wrap his brain around that nothingness, he grabbed the phone from the passenger seat and started to leave the Rabbit. He must have accidentally awakened the device, because there was the photo of Doug and Nell on the phone's screen, squished together so they'd fit into the camera's frame, making faces at him. He put the phone back to sleep, slipped it into his pocket, and headed for the D Star.

Wouldn't that be a joke, he said to himself as he climbed into the boat's cockpit: opening up the folding doors of the companionway and finding Nell laid out on the main saloon's cushions. Like, *Ha Ha! Surprise!* Yeah, that would be nice.

She wasn't there. But Trippy sat down there anyway, on the settee cushions, where she last had been, where he had made sure she recovered, where they had made love and argued and made up and eaten and slept and vowed and agreed and plotted. In the dark, he sat there, doing nothing, feeling lonely and numb and sorry and angry and pitiful with the lights turned off. It felt good, being depressed, because he was, profoundly, deeply. The thought of putting some music on crossed his mind, or maybe watching a Jenny film on the forty-inch TV, or maybe opening a bottle of wine if there was still any left onboard and drinking it all at once. So he could be depressed and drunk all at once. He did none of those things, but instead laid back into the cushions and stared up at the underside of the foredeck, out the hatch above him, into an inky black sky with no stars in it, wondering how long it would take for him to get over this. It wasn't such a tough one, not the toughest; he'd been worse off, and he'd recovered, moved on, pushing the present into the past, letting it spread and settle and smear and eventually blend in with all that stuff that made him him.

And then he started worrying about her, and fell asleep worried for her.

Consequence

Trippy's fitness watch told him it was after three in the morning. He didn't know why he had awakened, but suspected it was something to do with a guilty conscience. He should have had the wine. Would have slept through the night. Wouldn't have helped with the guilt, but at least he'd have the hangover to remind him to feel guilty.

Something wasn't right. Laying on his back in the main saloon, Trippy eyes were focusing on the black night framed by the hatch directly above him. He had done it hundreds of times before, lay there, the D Star in its slip, looking out, and be able to see the last foot or so of the mast of the boat slipped right next to the D Star, a Pearson thirty-two. Even at night. Because of the dock lights, the reflection. This night, in fact. He remembered it.

The mast wasn't there.

Trippy waited a moment, thinking it might dip back into the hatch's periphery. Maybe the tide or something. Or a wake from a boat. At three in the morning?

The view directly up and out the foredeck hatch remained inky dark.

So Trippy made the effort to prop himself up so he could look out one of the port side windows. Which was when he realized his boat was no longer in its slip. The orientation was all wrong. He was looking at the sterns of two other boats. In their respective slips. Where they should be. Just sitting there, not moving. But out the port side window? It could only mean that the D Star was in the middle of the slip channel, also just sitting there, not moving.

The boat on the right had the name *Munchkin* painted on it. Redman's boat.

Trippy bolted upright, jumped off the cushions and scrambled up the companionway steps. He froze on the third step of the companionway stairs.

The stern of the Munchkin was less than six feet away from the port side of the D Star.

Redman was standing on the stern of his boat, staring at Trippy, arms crossed, shaking his head.

"What the fuck is going on?" asked Trippy.

And at the same time that Redman jabbed a pointed finger towards the bow of the D Star, Trippy heard a voice, coming from that same direction.

"There's no fucking wind!"

It was Nell. She was at the bow, messing with the headsail which she had managed to unfurl, trying to splay it out in the hopes it would catch the whisper of wind coming over the boat's starboard stern.

Trippy sprang off the step and ran across the foredeck to join Nell at the bow.

"Nell!"

She turned around, clearly disappointed. "I wanted to surprise you."

"And what do you suppose I am right now?"

"Angry?"

Trippy threw his arms around her and lifted her off the deck. Then they kissed, a long hungry kiss that confirmed in Trippy's mind that he was in love with this girl – and the chameleon that came with her.

Nell pushed him away from the kiss.

"There's no time. We have to leave."

"Again?"

"For different reasons."

"Now what have you stolen?"

"Nothing like that. Come on, we'll use the engine." Nell took off towards the cockpit and added, "Now that you're awake."

Trippy followed her but stopped when he was abreast of Redman, still standing on the stern of his boat, arms still crossed. Trippy knew he had a stupid grin on his face, but couldn't help it, and didn't care.

"Who's that?" asked Redman.

"Are you kidding? That's her! Nell! The girl! The chameleon!"

"Doesn't look like her."

"She cut her hair. And changed the color. Besides, it's three in the morning."

"She a rock star? Another one of your secret rendezvous that you can't tell anyone about?"

"I'm telling you, that's the one who shot me!"

Trippy heard the D Star's engine come to life.

"Wasn't me," said Nell.

Redman smirked and kept his arms crossed. "As you pointed out, it's three o'clock in the morning Trippy. I know I'm your only neighbor, but you should still have some consideration for your neighbors. You and your rock stars and directors and big-wig software engineers. And movie stars. I know about the last one."

"What last one?"

Redman flapped his arms like a bird and cawed like a crow, then made a point of crossing his arms again. "I saw 'em. Both of 'em, when they were leaving the boat. Your boat. You're lucky I don't talk."

Trippy started to respond, but Redman held up a hand: the universal sign to stop. "Three o'clock in the morning, Trippy. Nearly four. I'm going back to bed." He then turned around and disappeared into the black of the Munchkin's below decks.

"Trippy!" It was Nell, a shouting whisper. "Come on!"

Trippy joined Nell in the cockpit as she eased the boat's transmission into forward gear from behind the starboard helm.

"I never should have taught you how to sail."

"Furl the jib," she said. "I can't see where we're going."

Trippy crossed to the port side of the cockpit and began reeling in the loop line that controlled the jib sail's furler.

"Where are we going, Nell?"

"Where do you want to go?"

"Back to sleep."

Nell cranked the wheel hard to starboard, pointing the D Star into the sterns of a collection of boats parked in their slips.

"Wrong answer!"

She straightened the boat out at the last second.

Trippy remained unruffled. "What's the right answer?"

"Anywhere with you, Nell, anywhere with you."

"Do I have to say it just like that? Like I'm gay?"

"What time is it?" she asked.

Trippy looked to his fitness watch. "A quarter to four in the morning."

Nell swore. "We're late."

"For what?"

"Do you trust me?"

"What's the catch?"

"There you go again. It's a yes or no question."

"Jesus Christ, there *you* go again."

"Yes or no."

"I'm in love with you."

"I'm guessing you're just not very good at games. In general."

"Not with you. Because I never win."

"You're winning now, aren't you?"

"I'm ahead. There's a difference."

Nell reached over and pushed the throttle until the boat speed was over five knots.

Trippy said, "We in a hurry?"

"Yep. How much longer til we're at the bridge?"

"Why. You got a date?"

"We do."

"With who?"

"Destiny."

Trippy reached over and pulled the throttle back to nothing.

Nell looked at him, like she didn't understand why he didn't understand. "We're escaping, Trippy." Said like, *won't this be fun! Another fun adventure!*

"From who?"

"Oh, now you want to know. Because before that didn't matter. Maybe it did. In fact, you definitely wanted to know. Which is what started all of our problems in the first place. Anyway, at this speed, you'll find out, because we won't escape."

"We?"

"You'll be sailing alone."

Trippy thought about that prospect for a moment, then reached over and pushed the throttle forward to over five knots boat speed.

Nell smiled. "I need a flashlight."

"Promise me you didn't steal anything this time."

"I'll say anything if you'll go get the fucking flashlight."

Trippy stayed right where he was.

Nell sighed and rolled her eyes. "I promise I didn't steal anything this time."

Trippy waited a moment to see if there was a second part to the promise, or a crack in her expression, or some other sign that she was lying. Nothing. She just kept smiling at him. So he went below to get the Duracell 1300. "Except for two million dollars in bitcoins. From my employer," Nell said under her breath.

Trippy returned and handed Nell the flashlight. Then she bunched her lips up and leaned in towards Trippy.

"What's the catch?" he asked. "Besides the two million in bitcoins."

Nell's jaw actually dropped. "I did not say that loud enough for you to hear me."

"Yes you did. I'll have to make a note in the ship's log. First time the girl ever let truth slip out of her lips." Trippy leaned in to Nell and finished the kiss she had started. And wished he'd taken a picture of the expression on her face.

Nell finally opened her eyes after the kiss ended. She then redirected her focus on the boat's course and steered the D Star closer to the starboard side of the channel.

"Take the wheel," she said.

Trippy did, and Nell headed forward with the flashlight. She stopped just ahead of the mast and began studying the starboard shoreline, like she was looking for something. The buildings lining the channel looked like some sort of storage facility, part of a larger shipping or freight holding complex: six giant silvery-white vertical cylinders, used to store something – probably unrefined fuel – and service roads and gates and perimeter fencing and two small windowless huts with yellow pipes exiting the cylinders, passing through the huts and then on to somewhere else further inland. A moment later Nell found whatever it was she was looking for, evidently, because she pointed the flashlight to the shore and blinked it on and off three times, deliberately.

Two seconds later, the music started, loud enough for Trippy and everyone else in the immediate area to know instantly what song it was before the singer even started singing: *The Cisco Kid*, by War. Seconds later a uniform string of lights popped on, and Trippy realized there were a row of cars parked head in, on one of those services roads, just at the edge of the water, on this side of a perimeter fence, their lights pointing out to the channel. Maybe twenty cars. And then he saw the people climbing out of the cars and walking towards the water's edge; just shapes and forms, really, silhouetted by car headlights. He was sure they were waving at the D Star.

He imagined they were wearing blue bandanas over their faces, but it was too dark to see.

Nell waved back once, then started dancing to the music, which carried over the water and beyond. It was the kind of dance you do when you're alone, the kind you do when you know no one's watching; uninhibited, free, natural, effortless. The kind of dance when you're celebrating your own private victory over something, when you're the only person who cares what it looks like because it's not about what it looks like, but how it makes you feel.

Horns started honking from the shore, and Trippy could hear people shouting, he didn't know what. Then the cars themselves started to dance, their beams of light skipping towards the sky then back to the water, the vehicles jumping up and down and rocking back and forth, the kind of dance you'd expect from a lowrider car.

The dancing and the lightshow went on for maybe half the song when suddenly everything stopped, abruptly, and without warning, the absence of it all rudely forcing the night back into place.

Two seconds later, the void was pierced by a burst of gunfire, a single eruption of many guns at once. Then another synchronized round, followed by a third and final chorus of shots a second later.

The silence, only briefly disturbed, returned. Trippy looked forward to Nell still standing on the foredeck, leaning out towards the water, one hand wrapped around the mast. She was looking right at him, and he was sure she was smiling. She then turned around and skipped up to the railing of the bow and leaned into it. She was looking up at something, and Trippy saw it was the Vincent Thomas Bridge, directly ahead of them. She raised the flashlight up and pointed it towards the bridge. A short moment later, three long and deliberate flashes of a single point of light came to the boat from up on the bridge. It was impossible for

Trippy to see the person who had sent the signal, but he had a good idea who it was.

They were beginning to pass under the bridge when Trippy abandoned his post at the wheel and went below. He fished the flash drive out of his pocket and plugged it into the boat's entertainment center USB port. He searched for the right song, pressed play, and returned to the cockpit.

Nell was still leaned in to the bow railing, looking directly up at the rim of the bridge as the D Star slowly passed underneath it. Then the music started playing. *The Cisco Kid*, performed by War.

Nell started dancing again.

And as Trippy watched a chameleon dance on the bow of a boat named D Star in the middle of the night on its way out to sea from a town called San Pedro (pronounced by the locals as *Peedro*, by the way) towards points unknown, he realized there was no escaping the fact that doing the right thing would always come with consequences.

He could live with that.

...from the London financial desk of CryptoNews Services...

Bitcoin Skyrockets after Hackers' Anonymous Gift
Dec 21, 2016 — 8:41PM EDT Updated: Dec 22, 2016 — 10:31AM EDT

Bitcoin spiked Wednesday as one of the largest exchanges reported an anonymous influx of nearly $250 million of the digital currency. Within minutes of opening, bitcoin values were trading nearly fifteen percent above the previous day's closing price. Trading was not halted.

Bitfinex confirmed to this source that an anonymous dump of $248 million mysteriously appeared on the exchange's servers without notice or explanation last night during what officials are calling a 'routine service update'.

"Obviously we're looking in to it," said Wendhall Gersh, a Bitfinex representative. "But it appears to be an actual gift from a group of hackers. It was not a technical error. Believe me, we've checked. Although the source is not yet verifiable, we were able to authenticate the transaction."

It was less than a month ago that the Bitfinex exchange and associated financial markets were roiled by the theft of nearly the same amount, $250 million, by what investigators believe was an anonymous hack. Officials are reluctant to concede the deposit was a return of the originally stolen money, but have not ruled out the possibility.

"Maybe somebody got a conscience," said a source who wished to remain anonymous. "Or maybe they considered the consequences and decided to do the right thing."

About the Author

Seneka Ecks is a lifelong sailor who sank his first sailboat all by himself at the tender age of 10, somewhere near Stinson Beach in the 60's. Seneka currently lives on a boat in Southern California with a winsome Labrador Retriever named Jib (but answers to "Dog") for a first mate, believes Catalina Island is perfect for weekend getaways, and has yet to sink anything else. This is his first novel.

Seneka welcomes all questions, comments and random thoughts about this book, all books, writing, sailing, people, boats of all kinds and life in general at
SenekaEcks@gmail.com.

And now, a brief preview of what's coming next from Seneka Ecks…

The
Human Structure

Prologue

In the stagnant cold and pervasive stillness of space, a perfect cube tumbled through the absence of light towards a star system lightyears from its point of origin. As it approached the system, the symmetrical object slowed its velocity and eased through a solar debris field encircling the relatively young collection of planets. When the cube reached the inner edge of the scattered plane of icy fragments, it paused: the targeted planet was slipping behind its host star.

The cube continued transmitting the recall signal.

There was no response.

~~~~~   ~~~~~

The man known as Paul Runyon, standing third in line for the teller window of the Wells Fargo branch on a cool and sunny mid-April morning in Bloomington, Minnesota, felt the cube's presence. The object was close; not here, not yet, but close. The cube's unique signal resonance had taken him by surprise, at first, like bumping into an old acquaintance while shopping for asparagus. It had been more than thirty years since he had last sensed the subtle vibration. Unmistakable nonetheless. The cube was calling to him, for him.

He would not answer.

~~~~~   ~~~~~

As the left crescent of the smeary white and blue sphere first appeared from behind its star, the cube measured its mass, orbital speed and gravitational relationships. It recalculated and verified the planet's time and distance to cube perihelion, then projected a correlated intercept trajectory to the planet's natural satellite.

It amplified the recall signal and continued transmitting.

~~~~~   ~~~~~

The man known as Paul Runyon sat by himself in the Caribou Coffee shop on the ground floor of the Tower building in Bloomington, enjoying delicate sips of a double espresso from a white china demitasse on a brilliantly clear and glorious June morning. The front page of the Financial Times was loaded on his digital tablet, but he wasn't reading it, pleasantly distracted by the obscured view of the lake across the street, Normandale Lake, on the other side of West Eighty-Fourth, with its tree-lined shores soaked in vibrant hues of green.

He needed the distraction. The cube's increase in signal strength was an irritant, like an allergy attack with its stuffy-headed headache, or the nagging presence of mosquitos, contemptuous of the desperate swat. Like an expensive divorce and the insatiable spouse who wanted it all, knowing that would never happen but going through the motions anyway, just because they could. Because the system allowed it, supported it, encouraged that kind of gratuitous greed. It was both wrong and proper. It was a necessity.

And yet the irritation was informative; he knew where the cube was in relation to him, to the planet, *his* planet. The sun had been in its way, between the cube and himself, requiring it to suspend the hunt. The increase in signal intensity was procedural, and revealed the planet was now in direct line with the cube. And he knew what the cube would next do, because he had failed to respond, what it had been programmed to do. He appreciated the cube's efficiency intimately, empathized with it for a disagreeable moment, and then synchronized his motivation to its actions. Now it was just a matter of time.

He knew the protocol.

If he did not respond to the recall signal, they would send a probe after him, a machine. The machine would attempt to link with him, to overwrite his neural network, to absorb him, to end his time – and his life – on Earth. He had prepared for this, had written structures to defend against it. As a drill, a theoretical scenario whose time to test had come. He would modify his Anonymity Structure and initiate a defense protocol; he would disappear from its sensors, disable the probe's keen ability to track him. The machine might even assume his demise, his destruction, and call off the hunt.

Not likely.

The man known as Paul Runyon began to cry, awkward and embarrassing tears leaking out and dripping down. It made no sense to him. He was human. He belonged here, amongst his people, his beloved people. It had no right. They had no right. He had the right, the right to continue living. He used a Caribou Coffee napkin to dab dry his face, then blew his nose. No one was close enough to have seen the breakdown.

He knew the protocol.

Once upon the threshold of the planet, the craft would generate a pulse, the mask that would confuse the Earth's tracking capabilities, allowing the cube to slip into the planet's atmosphere undetected, to land, to disembark, to begin the search. It was programmed to do just that.

The probe's capabilities exceeded all things human, yet was not human, and that would be his advantage. As hard as a machine tried, it would never perfectly emulate the human experience. Not without years and years of experiential training. The machine would be tasked with finding one particular human out of nearly eight billion. He would make sure there was nothing particular about him. The organic probe would be oblivious to his presence. Even if he were wrapped in its arms. The man known as Paul Runyon had six months to live, six months to prevent his death. He would succeed.

For the moment, the man known as Paul Runyon returned his attention to the espresso's aromatic suggestion of smoky-chocolate and began reading the digital version of his favorite morning paper. He wished he could have enjoyed the coffee while it was still hot.

~~~~~   ~~~~~

The cube, indifferently patient, remained in pause until the planet's orbit brought the engorged bluish ball of organic matter to the point closest to its location, its intercept trajectory within the debris field. The recall signal had remained unacknowledged and was now timed out. The cube terminated the focused broadcast and initiated a new protocol. The calculated path to the planet's natural satellite was implemented. The cube exited the debris field and accelerated toward the organic satellite.

Chapter One

The incessant chirping existed as something detached, an incongruous invasion of Keith Vetter's consciousness. He opened his eyes to blackness as the rhythmic set of pulsing beeps shoved a practical thought into his dream-soaked head. It was his mobile going off. His right arm was draped over Andrea's body and somehow a thickened twist of her fragrant hair had splayed itself over half his face.

The chirping continued.

His first thought was the consequences of the call waking Andrea. And then he remembered, this was Andrea, not his first wife, Ellen. That was how long it had been since receiving a call in the middle of the night. Ellen would have turned the interruption of her sleep into grounds for a trial separation. Andrea would be curious, at first, then sexually aroused when Vetter disconnected the call. What a difference twenty years and a thirty percent reduction in IQ made.

The chirping continued.

He delicately extricated himself from his someday-wife and looked to the faintly glowing digital clock on the same nightstand where his phone was. Two-fifty-four in the morning. He stayed in bed but picked up the phone and saw the name on the display: Lydecker, his deputy director at Jet Propulsion Laboratories. The chirping stopped. The name disappeared from the screen, replaced by three boxes stacked on top of each other, all telling him the same thing: missed calls from Lydecker. He had just returned the phone to the nightstand when it started chirping again.

He picked the device back up and tapped the accept icon, knowing what the call was about. "Jesus Christ, Pete."

"It's sitting behind the moon," said the deputy director. "It's just sitting there." His voice was low and sounded compressed, the way Pete Lydecker talked whenever stress got the better of him.

He was referring to a ghost, a chunk of bad data Lydecker had been chasing since the previous morning. Around ten AM that morning an orbiting space telescope had picked up an object departing the Kuiper Belt on a trajectory towards the planets. It was small and insignificant and would have gone unnoticed except that its speed was erratic. Over a period of about six hours, the delayed data streaming in from the Wide-Field Infrared Survey Explorer, or WISE space telescope recorded the object as both stationary and also moving at about one quarter the speed of light. Simultaneously. An hour later the telescope's onboard computers refused to admit there was ever anything there. No other component of the combined JPL/NASA deep space surveillance grid – ground or orbiting – was acknowledging the object. Lydecker and the WISE mission team had made it their goal to track down the source of the bad data.

Five hours later, the object was back, and had traveled over a billion miles in that time; theoretically possible, but practically absurd. Lydecker was beside himself, and in his heightened state of frustration, had suggested perhaps it was not bad data, that it might be something else. Vetter, the acting director of JPL, had pulled Lydecker into his office and behind closed doors offered the forty-year-old bachelor some patronizing advice. He was perhaps too close to the problem and may have lost a little of his otherwise grounded perspective on the matter. Were any of the other NASA deep space surveillance satellites reporting or tracking the object? No, confessed Lydecker. Had the data feed been consistent?

No. Had there been problems with the WISE data recently? Yes. So, what was the most probable scenario, he had asked his deputy director. Bad data, Lydecker admitted. Vetter then gave the man a reassuring shoulder squeeze and authorized him to continue working the problem, but suggested he take a couple steps back – and a break – before proceeding.

Around eight PM of that same evening, just as Vetter and Andrea were finishing an antipasto salad seated around the tiny kitchen table in their one-bedroom apartment, Lydecker had called to report the problem was solved. He had sounded relieved. They had run a full set of diagnostics on the WISE and everything was back to normal. There was no anomalous object, and perhaps never had been. Vetter had lauded Lydecker's tenacious approach to a thorny problem, congratulated him on the solution, and had suggested the deputy director call it a day. Or night.

Two hours later, ten o'clock at night, Lydecker, practically foaming at the mouth, called to report the WISE satellite just clocked the object passing Jupiter at well over fifty million KPS. He was working on the confirmation and would get back to Vetter. The call ended before Vetter uttered a word. The deputy director had sounded frantic, borderline hysterical. Vetter then made three successive phone calls; one to the WISE mission manager, at home but not yet asleep, who was acutely aware of the anomalous data, but willingly conceded the WISE data had been erratic for over a week now, and that they were working on it; one to the on-duty JPL security detail watch commander, asking him to personally and unofficially check in on Pete Lydecker; and one to Vivienne Hawley, director of human resources for JPL, who had just gone to bed, but was nonetheless grateful Vetter had given her a head's up about a potential HR situation, quickly developing, regarding the facility's deputy director.

Ten minutes later, Pete Lydecker called Vetter to apologize, deflated, admitting he had once again jumped the gun, that the WISE had returned to reporting no object at all, and that he was exhausted, done for the night, calling it quits, packing it in.

Vetter had suggested Pete take tomorrow off. Lydecker said he'd think about it.

And now this call, three in the morning. Lydecker had not gone home as promised. He had been at it for nearly twenty hours straight, chasing a phantom. The deputy director, someone Vetter would otherwise call a friend, was edging ever closer to an official reprimand, maybe even a write-up, definitely a preliminary psych evaluation. Vetter drew in a defeated breath, slowly exhaled, and asked again the same question he had been asking for nearly a day now. "Is it confirmed this time, Pete"?

"Yes," said Lydecker. "Six ground stations tracked it slipping behind the moon. Twenty-nine minutes ago. It hasn't moved." Vetter bolted upright in the bed. Andrea stirred. "The Lunar Reconnaissance Orbiter's gonna give us a visual on it in less than twelve minutes."

~~~~~   ~~~~~

Ellen, his first and only wife, would have never gotten out of bed in the middle of the night just to make Vetter a pot of coffee. Under any circumstance. Andrea was doing just that, wearing nothing but a pair of thong underwear, the black ones, in a waxing Southern California winter. The divorce had cost Vetter fifty-one percent of his retirement, and the girl making coffee practiced astrology. It was worth it.

He crossed to where the thirty-year old stood at the kitchen counter grinding coffee beans and used one hand to tuck in the white tag sticking out of the garment's whale tale. The other hand held the mobile to his ear, listening to Lydecker as he counted down the time before the Lunar Orbiter swung around the moon for a clear shot of the alien object... two minutes. STRATCOM had called in eighteen minutes ago, Lydecker continued, but it had been NORAD who suggested they classify the object as 'other', which was, in Lydecker's opinion, a bureaucratic misnomer... ninety seconds to live feed. Everyone who knew of the object's presence – which was, by now, an ever-widening circle of need-to-know insiders – was heartfelt-sure it was alien in nature, but no one dared use that word, including NORAD, for political reasons, so they called it an 'other'... sixty seconds. Lydecker had wanted to call Vetter half an hour earlier, knew he should have, but he had to be sure, considering the number of false alarms he'd already raised through the night. And when the military complex started calling, well, he got distracted, and... fifteen seconds.

The call went silent. Andrea handed Vetter coffee in a grey mug with the Libra astrological sign on it. Vetter took a sip, then tilted the mug to get a peek at the sweeping second hand of his wristwatch. It had been at least ten seconds.

"Pete?" he asked.

No response. Andrea positioned herself directly in front of Vetter and started playing with her nipples.

He heard Lydecker's voice, shouted and distant. "What? Say that again! What's happening, people! Somebody tell me what the fuck--" The call went quiet again. Precious seconds later Vetter heard, "Are you kidding me?" Sounded like a squeal. "What about Canberra? Check Madrid! Well check it again!"

"Pete!" said Vetter into the phone.

"They can't all be down! Jesus Christ, people!" Lydecker was in full panic and not bothering with his boss on the phone.

"Pete! Godamn it! Calm yourself and tell me what the fuck is going on!" shouted Vetter, the exclamation jolting Andrea's attention, her nipples reflexively hardening.

He heard what sounded like panting breaths on the phone. "We have no downlink," said Lydecker. An agonized whine. "Nothing. Everything's down. Across the board. Goldstone, Canberra, Madrid, every single dish has gone offline. We're blind. We're fucking blind." More airy breaths over the phone's speaker, then Lydecker said, "You better get down here, Keith--" The call disconnected abruptly. Vetter tried twice to redial the call before seeing the notification on the face of his phone: SEARCHING FOR SERVICE.

Chapter Two

The frequencies alteration had a rippling effect on the surface of his thought process and Paul Runyon knew. Goosebumps formed on the skin of his forearms with the temperature inside the Super Walmart steady at seventy degrees. It almost felt good. He parked the shopping cart containing a selection of fresh vegetables, frozen entrees and a canister of steel-cut oatmeal next to a twelve-foot freezer unit filled with cellophane-wrapped packets of sale-priced Farmer John's pork link sausages. One by one, he removed the items from his cart and placed them on top of the chilled pork links inside the refrigerated display.

He then pushed the empty shopping cart out of the grocery section, past the aisles of shoes and diapers and beyond the walls of flatware and televisions but made a left into a corridor when he saw the laundry detergent. He placed four one-gallon jugs of Great Value bleach into the cart. Nine feet farther down and on the aisle's opposing side, he found as many gallon-jugs of ammonia and placed those in the cart as well. He then weaved and wheeled the cart across the hundred thousand square-foot store until arriving at the gardening department tucked into a corner of the building. He found a three-gallon weed sprayer with a wand nozzle made by a company called Hudson and placed that in the shopping cart. As he purchased the items with cash at a self-checkout register, the spectrum of altered frequencies abruptly jiggled back into an acceptable range. The anomaly had lasted seven minutes, eleven seconds. That alone was conviction enough. It was fourteen minutes past five a.m. as he exited the super store through two sets of slithering glass doors. He initiated an exit sequence for his current location of Minneapolis.

The frequencies alteration was dispersed, per Infiltration Structure protocol. He had sensed it washing over the planet, wrapping around its spherical curve to form a hermetic seal of electromagnetic interference. Seven minutes, eleven seconds. He was smiling as he wheeled the shopping cart of supplies through the Walmart parking lot to the trunk of a black Jaguar XJ.

The cube had arrived. It was on the planet.

He started the supercharged V6 engine by pressing a button while seated on leather upholstery and knew he liked this car. And the townhouse on Penn Avenue with its view out the south-facing living room windows of a tree-studded park; and its swimming pool and built-in barbecue stands and fitness center and free WiFi. He liked being comfortable and human and eternal and having sex with females who sighed with urgent pleasure in his ear. He preferred the females and their organic energy, purple waves of it, soaking and gushing and vibrating and penetrating him with instinctive sincerity. Humans, with their tendency towards neural unpredictability that challenged his structural protocols, forcing them – and him – to adapt. Stimulus. It was all about stimulus. He would preserve his own integrity because that was what his instructions told him to do.

~~~~~   ~~~~~

"It was all a drill."

"Yes."

"You want me to go out there and tell the entire staff of JPL that the seven minutes and eleven seconds of downlink interruption was a planned event."

"A test. You know, like the emergency broadcast system."

"That is not going to happen."

"It has to. It will be more palpable, coming from you."

"Do you mean palatable?"

"No."

"What about the object six of our ground stations and at least one intel-secure satellite monitored slipping behind the moon and parking there for nearly half an hour?"

The man's smile was shallow. "What object? Your Lunar reconnaissance satellite is currently providing a live feed of the backside of the moon. Nothing but impact scars and craters. Barren land. Business as usual. And we've secured all of your data files. You'll get them back. Once we've reviewed them."

The realization that they had assumed complete control of his facility in less than thirty minutes did more than annoy Keith Vetter; it frightened him. He had quickly dressed and was in the car not five minutes after the call with Lydecker had gone dead. And at that time of day – not yet four AM – there was no traffic on the eighteen-mile drive from the apartment in Glendora to the Jet Propulsion Laboratories complex in La Canada, California. He had broken a good variety of traffic laws to get there only to find the usual field gate security detail replaced with camouflaged soldiers in helmets and body armor, flat-black automatic weapons slung over their shoulders and at the ready. He had been badged four separate times before being permitted to enter the building where his office was located. There had been more military personnel stationed inside. Two of them strapped with side arms had silently escorted Vetter across the building's lobby, up three floors in an elevator and down the hallway to his office – at least four minutes without a word spoken – only to discover these two strangers in his office.

Vetter smirked and said with a controlled voice, "It was there. We all saw the evidence. It's undeniable." No reaction from the man. Vetter threw his hands in the air and paced back and forth on the cramped stretch of gray industrial carpet in front of his desk, the desk he was prevented from sitting behind because the unshaven man in a suit with no tie was sitting there, a foot perched on the edge of his desk. He didn't even know his name. Or the other guy's, the older one, standing behind the desk, also in a suit, his back to Vetter, looking out the window through louvred blinds.

Vetter stopped pacing and turned back to the one seated. "These people aren't idiots, you know. They're trained scientists, doctors in astrophysics, PhD's in aeronautical engineering. They'll never believe this was a drill. The EM disruption blanketed the whole world. Billions of people went without cable TV or WiFi, or satellite radio, GPS, god knows what. Seven minutes! Exactly what kind of drill is that? Do you not understand the scope of this event?"

"You'll convince them they were part of a top-secret military experiment. A successful one," said the man at the window without turning around. "One that they'll keep their mouths shut about or they'll lose more than just their security clearance. We'll handle the cable TV problem."

Vetter was dumbfounded. He glared at the man seated. "You guys knew about this?"

"We never said that," said the man at the desk.

"We want you to say it," said the man at the window. He turned around and looked at Vetter. Older than Vetter by about ten years, maybe late fifties. His appearance was polished, professional, neatly clipped graying hair, starched white shirt under a navy-blue suit – also minus the tie. This one had managed to shave recently.

"What about the object?" challenged Vetter. "The one that somehow obtained point-two lightspeed before stopping at our moon?"

"You mean the simulation?" said the man seated at the desk.

"Don't bullshit me! That was no simulation."

"You'll tell them it was, and that you knew all about it," said the man standing. He was patronizing Vetter with a practiced smile. "Look, I know," he continued, "this is the point in time where you make an ethical stance and say something like, 'what if I don't', or 'you can't make me', 'I'm not going along with this'; something like that. But I think you know better. I think you know I have the authority to end your life, or promote you, or completely ignore you and just walk away. All three of those options are available to me." The condescending smile came back for a moment.

"But let's try some positive reinforcement this time. How about you get back the majority of your retirement package. You know, the one you gave away to that bitch Ellen. And we'll make sure Andrea's husband stays locked up in San Quentin for, what – another twenty years? Would that work for you?"

Vetter was unaware his mouth had fallen open.

The man seated at Vetter's desk chuckled. "Look at that. He didn't know she was married."

The patronizing smile returned to the man standing. "So, what do you say, Keith, you with us on this?"

~~~~~   ~~~~~

Lydecker had been standing three doors down in the middle of the junction of two hallways of the fourth floor of JPL's 800 building, looking nervous and exhausted and frightened, waiting, for nearly fifteen minutes before seeing Vetter exit his office alone. He walked quickly towards the facility director, intercepted him, and looked both directions down the hallway to ensure they were outside the ears of the posted MPs. "This is not good, Keith, not good at all."

"Yeah, well, it's about to get worse."

"Is that possible?"

"Get everyone together in Building 321. The auditorium. GS-3 clearance and up, facility wide. Everyone."

"But it's not even six AM."

"Just do it. We have an announcement to make."

"We?" asked Lydecker.

Made in the USA
Monee, IL
15 July 2024